I0640760

David Forbes

True Story of the Christiana Riot

David Forbes

True Story of the Christiana Riot

ISBN/EAN: 9783337259297

Printed in Europe, USA, Canada, Australia, Japan

Cover: Foto ©Andreas Hilbeck / pixelio.de

More available books at **www.hansebooks.com**

A TRUE STORY

OF THE

CHRISTIANA RIOT.

꩜

By DAVID R. FORBES,

Editor of The Quarryville Sun.

LIBRARY.

QUARRYVILLE, PA. :

THE SUN PRINTING HOUSE,

1898.

It is not well,
Here in this land of Christian liberty,
That honest worth or hopeless want should dwell
Unaided by our care and sympathy.

—Phœbe Carey.

COPYRIGHT, 1898,
BY THE SUN PRINTING HOUSE,
QUARRYVILLE, PA.

TO

THE SOCIETY OF FRIENDS,

WHOSE

SYMPATHIES AND ASSISTANCE

WERE

ALWAYS TENDERED TO THE PERSECUTED,

THIS WORK

IS

REVERENTLY DEDICATED

BY

THE AUTHOR.

We live in deeds, not years—in thoughts, not breaths—
In feelings, not in figures on a dial ;
We should count time by heart-throbs. He most lives,
Who thinks most—feels the noblest—acts the best.

—BAILEY.

PREFACE.

THIS work is, perhaps, more the offspring of love for local history, than the belief that it is a necessity. Entire originality is not claimed ; therefore, while much, to the general reader, will be new, no doubt some passages will be found familiar, and, like old friends, it is hoped their reappearance will be hailed with pleasure.

In its preparation the most serious consideration has been given to truthfulness. Neither time nor labor has been spared to verify the statements herein contained. The ground has been critically examined, old residents interviewed, and the story as published in THE QUARRYVILLE SUN has withstood the censure of a discriminating public and received only words of praise. On the strength of this it is now presented in a more convenient and less perishable form.

Should the perusal of this volume awaken the latent interest of even one young man of to-day, and encourage him to jot down his recollections of neighboring folk-lore for the enlightenment of future generations, the author will feel amply repaid for the time and care which have been bestowed on this and similar articles.

In conclusion, allow me to say, that I have freely availed myself of the labors of the best authorities, and it is largely due to the researches of my friend Mrs. Philena C. Jackson, that I have been able to gather and verify much that makes this work valuable as a book of reference for the local historian in the years to come.

QUARRYVILLE, PA.   D. R. F.
        January, 1898.

What is life?
'Tis not to stalk about, and draw fresh air
From time to time, or gaze upon the sun:
'Tis to be free.   When liberty is gone,
Life grows insipid, and has lost its relish.

—ADDISON.

THE CHRISTIANA RIOT.

WHEN the bill known as the "Fugitive Slave Law" was passed during Taylor's administration in 1850, perhaps no more unsavory measure was ever forced on the American people—but more especially heavy was the burden on the peaceful and law-abiding residents of southern Chester and Lancaster counties. The population here was largely of the Quaker element—a people noted for their opposition to slavery in any of its forms. These counties, bordering on Maryland, the most northern slave state, had become famous through their system of "underground railways," as they were called, and many an old slave owed his life and freedom to the good people who "passed" him from hand to hand and furnished food and clothing for the emergency.

The provisions of this infamous act were that any one assisting, harboring or giving aid to any fugitive slave should be deemed guilty of a misdemeanor and subject to a penalty of not more than six months imprisonment and pay a fine of $1,000. The government was also to pay $1,000 for each slave who was lost to his master. It was further provided that any one called upon by a deputy marshal to assist in the capture of a runaway slave was required to act in that capacity and do the bidding of his superior officer, whether right or wrong. Even the giving of food to a black man made the donor a subject for prosecution when an over-zealous official wished to display his authority or create consternation among the colored residents of any particular locality.

Numerous meetings were held and the law roundly de-
nounced. One stalwart Abolitionist made the remark that "it
is a statute which tramples on Justice, outrages all true rever-
ence for Law, assails the dearest rights and holiest instincts of
men, which virtually outlaws a large class of our population
and sets at defiance the laws of God." It gave the slaveholder the excuse for a grand slave hunt throughout neighboring states, which he enjoyed more than the people of to-day
would a fox hunt or a horse race. It gave to the unprincipled
deputy marshals the "open sesame" to the homes of the colored residents, which they could ravage and plunder at will,
and many an innocent girl, or able-bodied young man was
kidnaped and sold from the auction block in the South.

Josiah Pickel, of Bart township, recalls one of the disgraceful
incidents which were quite common in those days. When he
lived with his father, Peter Pickel, on what is now known as
the Hugh Fulton farm along the Valley road, a colored man
lived with his family in John McGowen's house, the adjoining
place, where Miller Mendenhall now lives. The negro was a
post and railer by trade and very industrious. One evening
after dusk a couple of men in a wagon drove up to his house
and asked his wife if John was home. She replied that he was
not, but was working for a neighbor and probably was coming
up the road. They drove away and met him, talked for a
while, and one knocked him down and then threw him into
the wagon when they drove rapidly away. A scream, when he
was attacked, was the last that his wife and family ever heard
from him, and no doubt a large sum was received for him by
his captors in some southern market. This is only one of the
hundreds of such cases of the stealing of human beings at
which the unscrupulous made a living, and there are several
people still surviving, unless wrongly accused, who accumulated much of their wealth in this questionable manner.

With such a state of affairs in existence, is it any wonder
that the culmination should have been otherwise than it were?

The Pennsylvania "Freeman" in speaking of the Riot said: "Deplorable as it is in 'its character, and many of its results, the calm and candid thinker cannot fail to see that it has grown legitimately—necessarily—from the passage and the attempt to enforce the cruel and disgraceful provisions of National law. What right has the American nation to expect anything else from its own teachings, and its own actions? Have they not proclaimed "Liberty or death;" "Resistance to tyrants is duty to God," as their National creed? Have they not honored and rewarded the daring and exploits of the battle-ground as true heroism? Rebellion or flight is the slave's only hope of freedom. The government now lets loose its minions upon them, refuses them the shelter of the law, gives its law as an engine of cruelty into the hands of the man-hunters. What wonder that, outlawed as they are, they think it no crime for them to defend their liberties by the same means, for using which the "revolutionary heroes" of our own and other countries are glorified?"

Spies and informers were everywhere. Our state had been the chosen hunting-ground of the slaveholder for a year or more. Every peaceful valley, as well as populous town, was infested with prowling kidnapers on the watch for their prey. It is said that Pennsylvania furnished more victims than any other two states of the Union to the detestable Fugitive Slave law. Quiet homes and peaceful communities were constantly threatened with midnight incursions of man-hunters, with their treacheries, stratagems, their ruffian outrages and bloody violence, and menacing the defenseless people of color with a "reign of terror."

CHAPTER II.

THE RESULT.

THE first suit in southern Pennsylvania under the Fugitive Slave law, was brought against a man named Kauffman, whose family had given food and shelter to a lot of negroes entirely unbeknown to the farmer. He was indicted under all the charges, and suit was also brought against him for the full value of the slaves thus aided to escape. Thaddeus Stevens was engaged to defend Mr. Kauffman and the case came up before the United States Court at Philadelphia. Eminent counsel were employed on both sides and the legal fight was long and bitter, but finally the case went to the jury. The excitement ran high. One day, three days, a week, two weeks, four weeks went by and no verdict had been reached. Abraham N. Cassel, of Marietta, was on that jury, and he "hung" for six weeks, or until a verdict in favor of the slaveholder was prevented, and Kauffman acquitted.

That the fatal slave-hunt, which afterward became famous as the Christiana Riot, had been deliberately planned and was to be executed by strategem and violence was brought to light at the time of the inquest by the finding of the following letter upon the body of Mr. Gorsuch :

Lancaster. CO. 28 *August* 1851

Respected friend, I have the required
Information of four men that is within
Two miles of each other.   now the best
Way is for you to come as A hunter
Disguised about two days ahead of your son and let him come
    by way of Philadelphia and get the deputy marshal John
    Nagle I think is his name.   tell him the situation
And he can get force of the right kind it will take
About twelve so that they can divide and take them

All within half an hour.   now if you can come on the 2d or 3d
   of September come on & I will
Meet you at the gap when you get their
Inquire for Benjamin Clay's tavern let
Your son and the marshal get out
Kinyer's* hotel now if you cannot come
At the time spoken of write very soon
And let me know when you can
I wish you to come as soon as you possibly can
   Very respeetfully thy friend
                    WILLIAM M. P.
         [In pencil]   *Wm M Padgett.*

On the next page several memoranda were written in pencil,
probably by the slaveholder himself, of the times of the cars,
and the names of persons in the neighborhood of the scene of
the affray, with whom it was supposed colored men resided,
together with the following :

            Robert M Lee
   John Agen Henry H. Cline
            Depatised
         Marshal Kline
         Lawyer Lee
         and Benit
         Commissioner
         Ingraham
   O. Riley's Telegraph
         avoid Halzel
         Councelman
         Cpt Shutt
         J R Henson

The letter was directed to " Mr. Edward Gorsuch, Hereford
P. O., Balt. Co M. D." and postmarked at " Penningtonville
(now Atglen), Pa., Aug. 29, 1851." It also revealed the
miserable creature who sold himself as informer in the case.
He was a young man bred in the neighborhood, but who had
resided for some years in Baltimore, and from his habits had
peculiar opportunities to ascertain the residence, and worm
himself into the confidence, of the colored people.

---

                 * Kinzey's.

CASTNER HANWAY.

Padgett is still remembered by the older inhabitants of the neighborhood as a peripatetic, who traveled over the country fixing clocks as a cloak for his intrigues. By this means he was enabled to get into all the houses, and his keen insight into human nature taught him where to look for his unsuspecting victims. During the fall months he pretended to be gathering sumac tops for the dyeing of morocco. By these means he became aware of every cow path and by-road, and could keep a close watch wherever he suspected a victim might be concealed and thus make an accurate report to his chief, Kline, who soon became known as "the notorious slave-catching constable."

The scene of this conflict, which might almost be regarded as the first battle of the great Civil War, is about half a mile south of the Valley road, and perhaps some two and a-half miles southwest from Christiana, on the farm now owned by Marion Griest, and at that time the property of Levi Pownall. Notwithstanding the fact that almost fifty years have passed, the orchard surrounding the house where the tragedy occurred is in a remarkably healthy condition, while the old stone house which one should have thought would be preserved for generations is fast crumbling to dust in an unsuccessful attempt to battle against the elements.

At that time this spot must have been an ideal one for seclusion, situated as it is near a fourth of a mile from any public highway, and standing well up on the northern slope of a hill, surrounded by trees, being almost invisible to the outside world, yet in such a position that the ever-alert resident could clearly scan the surrounding country for a long distance, and note the approach of suspicious characters in time to avert any impending danger to the inmates. Such was the stronghold where the first and last battle of a terrible conflict was fought and won by the colored people in Lancaster county.

·CHAPTER III.

WAR.

THIS account of the affray is taken from the papers of September 18th, the week following the tragedy.'

On Thursday morning (the 11th of September, 1851) a peaceable neighborhood in the borders of Lancaster county was made the scene of a bloody battle, resulting from an attempt to capture seven colored men as fugitive slaves.

Very early on the morning of the 11th inst. a party of slave-hunters went into a neighborhood about two miles west of Christiana, near the eastern border of Lancaster county, in pursuit of fugitive slaves. The party consisted of Edward Gorsuch, his son Dickerson Gorsuch, his nephew Dr. Pearce, Nicholas Hutchins and two others, all from Baltimore county, Md., and one Henry H. Kline a notorious slave-catching constable from Philadelphia who had been deputized by Commissioner Ingraham for this business. At about day-dawn they were discovered lying in ambush near the house of William Parker, a colored man, by an inmate of the house who had started for his work. He fled back to the house pursued by the slave-hunters, who entered the lower part of the house, but were unable to force their way into the upper part to which the family had retired. A horn was blown from an upper window, two shots were fired, both by the assailants, one at the colored man who fled into the house, and the other at the inmates through the window. No one was wounded by either. A parley ensued. A slaveholder demanded his slaves, which he said were concealed in the house. Three colored men presented themselves successively at the window and asked if they were the slaves claimed. Gorsuch said that neither of them was his slave. They told him they were the only colored men in the house and warned him and his party to leave, as they were determined never to be taken alive as slaves. Soon the colored people from the neighborhood, alarmed by the horn, began to gather, armed with guns, axes, corn-cutters and clubs. Mutual threatenings were uttered by the two parties. The slave-hunters told the blacks that resistance would be useless, as they had a party of thirty men in the woods near by. The blacks warned them again to leave, as they would die before they would go into slavery.

From an hour to an hour and a-half passed in these parleyings, angry conversations and threats, the blacks increasing by new arrivals until they probably numbered from thirty to fifty; most of them armed in some way. About this time Castner Hanway, a white man and a Friend, who resided in the neighborhood, rode up and was soon followed by Elijah Lewis, another Friend, a merchant in Cooperville — both gentlemen highly esteemed as worthy and peaceable citizens. As they came up Kline, the deputy marshal, ordered them to aid him as a United States officer to capture the fugitive slaves. They refused, of course—as would any man not utterly destitute of honor, humanity and moral principle—and warned the assailants that it was madness for them to attempt to capture fugitive slaves there, or even to remain, and begged them, if they wished to save their own lives, to leave the ground.

Kline replied, "Do you really think so?" "Yes," was the answer, "the sooner you leave the better, if you would prevent bloodshed." Kline then left the ground, retiring a very safe distance into a cornfield and toward the woods. The blacks were so exasperated by his threats that, but for the interposition of the two white Friends, it is very doubtful whether he would have escaped without injury.

Messrs. Hanway and Lewis both exerted their influence to dissuade the colored people from violence, and would probably have succeeded in restraining them had not the assailing party fired upon them. Young Gorsuch asked his father to leave, but the old man refused, declaring, it is said and believed, that he would "go to hell or have his slaves."

Finding they could do nothing further, Hanway and Lewis both started to leave, again counseling the slave-hunters to go away and the colored people to peace, but had gone but a few rods when one of the inmates of the house attempted to come out at the door. Gorsuch presented his revolver, ordering him back. The colored man replied, "You had better go away if you don't want to get hurt," and at the same time pushed him aside and passed out. Maddened at this, and stimulated by the question of his nephew, whether he would "take such an insult from a d—d nigger," Gorsuch fired at the colored man and was followed by his son and nephew, who both fired their revolvers. The fire was returned by the blacks, who made a rush upon them at the same time. Gorsuch and his son fell, the one dead, the other wounded. The rest of the party, after firing their revolvers, fled precipitately through the corn and to the woods, pursued by some of the blacks. One was wounded, the rest escaped unhurt. Kline, the deputy marshal, who boasted of his miraculous escape from a volley of musket balls, had kept at a safe distance, though urged by young Gorsuch to stand by his father and protect him, when he refused to leave the ground. He of course came off unscathed. Several colored men were wounded, but none very severely. Some had their hats or their clothes perforated with bullets; others were slightly grazed and others had flesh wounds. They said that the Lord protected them, and they shook the bullets from their clothes. One man found several shot in his boot, which seemed to have spent their force before reaching him and did not even break the skin.

The slave-hunters having all fled several neighbors, mostly Friends and anti-slavery men, gathered to succor the wounded and take charge of the dead.

It is said that Parker himself protected the wounded man

from his excited comrades and brought water and a bed from his own house for the invalid, thus showing that he was as magnanimous to his fallen enemy as he was brave in the defense of his own liberty.

The young man was then removed to a neighboring house, where the family received him with the tenderest kindness and paid him every attention, though they told him in Quaker phrase that "they had no unity with his cruel business" and were very sorry to see him engaged in it. He was much affected by their kindness and expressed his regret that he had been thus engaged, and his determination, if his life was spared, never again to make a similar attempt.

CHAPTER IV.

THE SEQUEL.

ALL attempts to procure assistance to capture the fugitive slaves failed, the people in the neighborhood either not relishing the business of slave-catching, or at least not choosing to risk their lives in it. There was a very great reluctance felt to going even to remove the body, and the wounded man, until several Abolitionists and Friends had collected for that object, when others found courage to follow.

Deputy Attorney Thompson, of Lancaster, was there on Friday afternoon and issued warrants upon the deposition of Kline and others for the arrest of all suspected persons. A company of police were scouring the neighborhood in search of colored people, several of whom were seized while at their work near by and brought in.

Castner Hanway and Elijah Lewis, hearing that warrants were issued against them, went to Christiana and voluntarily gave themselves up, calm and strong in the confidence of their innocence. They, together with the arrested colored men, were sent to Lancaster jail that night.

The next morning the ground of the battle and the family where young Gorsuch lay were visited. He had just made a deposition to the effect that he believed no white persons were engaged in the affray beside his own party. As he was on the ground during the whole controversy, and Deputy Marshal Kline had discreetly run off into the corn-field before the fighting began, the hireling slave-catcher's eager and confident testimony against the whites weighed lightly with impartial men.

On returning to Christiana it was found that the U. S. marshal from the city had arrived at that place, accompanied by Commissioner Ingraham; Mr. Jones, a special commissioner of the United States from Washington; U. S. District Attorney Ashmead with forty U. S. marines from the navy yard, and a posse of about forty of the city marshal's police, together with a large body of special constables—men eager for such a manhunt—from Columbia and Lancaster, and other places. This crowd divided into parties of from ten to twenty-five and scoured the country in every direction for miles around, ransacking the houses of the colored people, and captured every colored man they could find, with several colored women, and two other white men.

That our readers may have some idea of the sentiments of the press at that time, we quote a few extracts. The " North American" said :

"There can be no difference of opinion concerning the shocking affair which occurred at Christiana on Thursday— the resisting of a law of Congress by a band of armed negroes, whereby the majesty of the government was defied and life taken in one and the same act. There is something more than a mere ordinary, something more than even a murderous riot in all this. It is an act of insurrection; we might, considering the peculiar class and condition of the guilty parties, almost call it a servile insurrection, if not also one of treason. Fifty—eighty or a hundred—persons, whether white or black, who are deliberately in arms for the purpose of resisting the law—even the law for recovering fugitive slaves—are in the attitude of levying war against the United States; and doubly heavy becomes the crime of murder in such a case, and doubly serious the accountability of all who have any connection with the act as advisers, suggesters, countenancers or accessories in any way whatever."

The "Sun" said :

" The unwarrantable outrages committed last week at

Christiana, in Lancaster county, is a foul stain upon the fair name and fame of our state. We are pleased to see that the officers of the Federal and State governments are upon the tracks of those who were engaged in the riot, and that several arrests have been made. We do not wish to see the poor, misled blacks, who participated in the affair, suffer to any very great extent—for they were but tools. The men who are really chargeable with treason against the United States government, and with the death of Mr. Gorsuch, an estimable citizen of Maryland, are unquestionably white, with hearts black enough to incite them to the commission of any crime equal in atrocity to that committed in Lancaster county. Pennsylvania has now but one course to pursue—and that is, to aid, and warmly aid, the United States in bringing to condign punishment every man engaged in the riot."

CHAPTER V.

THE TESTIMONY AT THE HEARING.

IN the previous chapters the reader has been made acquainted with the causes that led to the riot. He has been taken over the ground of the affray and left with the United States marshal and other officials at Christiana. We will now proceed with the testimony, as given before Commissioner Ingraham. That some of it was either shockingly warped by prejudice and excitement, or was the coinage of malicious perjury, there is not the slightest doubt. Nothing could have been more false than the charge as was shown.

Miller Knott affirmed : Resides close to where the transaction occurred in Sadsbury township; was not present when it occurred—I mean the resistance of the law and the murder of Gorsuch; there was no one with deceased when I saw him first; there were many colored people there, between seventy-five and one hundred; knew Isaiah Clarkson for one, Ezekiel Thompson, a boy named Samuel Booth; saw some white people there; knew Elijah Lewis and Joseph Scarlett; can't think of any others; Clarkson was not armed, the others had clubs; the man shot was on his horse in the lane when I saw him; had no conversation with Scarlett, except when I assisted to carry deceased to Mr. Pownall's house; the crowd had not altogether dispersed; Scarlett expressed no opinion when he carried deceased; no report about arresting the blacks; saw no officers that I know of; the one we took in was the son of deceased; the old gentleman, dead, was lying in the lane; the firing took place after the sun was up some time; a good many guns or pistols were fired; saw a man riding off armed on horseback; the firing was principally from black men; there was hallooing before the firing; did not hear a horn blow; Scarlett lives about one and a-half miles from the place; he was riding out of the lane and had been there before me; after awhile I saw him ride in again; the main body of the firing was over; he must have passed within ten yards of where the man was wounded; there was no conversation between us that I recollect; I knew that William Parker lived there and that Pinckney did, also; Clarkson was there; had no conversation with any person that did approve of the firing.

John Knott affirmed : I live with my father; am going on fourteen years; remember the killing of Mr. Gorsuch; it was a little after the sun was up when the firing commenced; I went over and looked at him from the fence where the battle was; just above the house there were a good many people, many blacks; about seventy-five or ninety black people; many of them were armed; saw no white people that I knew; I knew some of the black people—Zekiel Thompson was one, Samuel Smith was another, and one Jackson; that's all I know; they were firing while I stood at the fence and looked over; saw the old gentleman who was killed after he was dead; he lay a little piece from the house in the lane; did not see him fall; saw the young man that was wounded; saw him led out of the lane by another man; Parker and Pinckney lived there; saw Parker after the fight was over, he came out of the house and was talking with a white man; don't know who he was; saw the young man carried over to Mr. Pownall's house; saw Scarlett there with the wounded man; when I first saw Scarlett it was when the wounded man was lying by the side of the fence; heard Scarlett talking with several of the people about there— white people; was not near enough to hear anything he said; went over before my father went to this place; saw that Scarlett's horse was hitched to the fence, went home, got my breakfast, came back, and then I saw his horse; they were standing not very far from the door when they fired; was told by Tamsey Brown that a colored man took money from the old man killed; the money was brought in and divided among the women, Abraham Johnson keeping a portion of it himself.

Tamsey Brown sworn : Live one mile from Penningtonville with my grandmother; was at school and don't remember when the man was killed; was at school the day he was killed; know where Parker's house is; was never at his place; the name of the man who lived with Parker was Pinckney; when I came from school first, heard the man was killed from grandmother; don't know what became of the money about the man killed; did not tell any one that I did; knew Hannah Pinckney and Eliza Parker, who lived in that house; heard talk of it; young Knott was speaking to me when we were coming up the lane; he asked if I did not wish the men had staid home; I did not say anything then; did not tell the lad that the man Johnson came in with a handful of money; know Abraham Johnson, who used to live with Pinckney in the stone house; have not seen him this week, don't know where he is now; don't know my age; Susan Clarkson is my grandmother; can't read.

George Washington Harvey Scott sworn : Live with John Kerr; was present when the man was killed, but had no hand in it; was there over night and staid out of doors in the road; there was no one with me; was persuaded to go over by John Morgan and Henry Simms, colored men; did not tell me what they wanted me to go over for; saw them both there, out by the door of the house; they had arms; there was a good many colored people there; did not see any but Morgan and Simms that I knew; saw them shoot—saw the old gentleman shot; he fell in the lane; he was shot by Henry Simms; did not see the nephew shot, neither did I see the son fall, for there was such a crowd; have seen Scarlett, but don't know him; he was not there; saw no white man except Castner Hanway, the miller; John Morgan cut the old gentleman in the head with a corn-cutter after he (Mr. Gorsuch) had fallen; this was after sunrise; went away as soon as the old man was killed; I left the other colored people there; they had pistols, muskets, and other guns; they wanted me to help, but I would have nothing to do with it; that is, in taking their part in the fight, which was to kill the slaveholders; did not understand who they were coming there to take; the mob was to resist all slaveholders; the firing came from the house, down stairs; heard a horn blow —the fight was beginning then; it was blown from the house; the horn continued to blow right on; the firing at first came in a body, and continued on then more and more; it then became scattering; after the horn was blown they began to assemble pretty quick.

John Criley sworn : Reside at Penningtonville; have lived in the neighborhood twelve years; know where Mr. Parker's house is; don't know Parker; know Mr. Scarlett; have known him for the last seven years; he is a farmer and resides about three quarters of a mile from Parker's house; recollect the time when the murder occurred at Parker's house and was there about 9 o'clock the same morning; I was told that Scarlett had been riding about in the morning, and told the negroes to attend to that place; Henry Murr, the blacksmith, told me; he said that Scarlett had been riding round, to the best of his knowledge, notifying the negroes.

Henry Cloud sworn : Don't know anything about Morgan having been there; the day before the murder I told him some people were up for slaves, and asked him if he was going out; he said he was going out that night, and my understanding was that he intended to resist the process in taking the slaves; don't know that he was out that night.

Henry H. Kline sworn : I thought I saw Scarlett coming from the scene of the murder upon a horse; he was in a hurry, but was not at the place at the time of the firing; I said, you are the man that gave the warning; asked him to stop, telling him that a man was dead up the road, and asked him where the nearest doctor was; he gave us no answer; told him the negroes had killed him, but he made no reply, and drove on;

PARKER'S HOUSE, 1851.

he was then dressed differently from what he now is; we
started for Parker's house on Wednesday morning, and got
there a little after daylight—Mr. Gorsuch, son, nephew, and
three others whose names I don't know; some fifty yards from
the house we met one of the blacks who had come out of the
house down the lane, towards us; as soon as he was espied he
returned and ran to the house, and I after him; the old gentleman and one of his sons took to the field to head him off ; the
black got into the house and upstairs before I got up; as soon
as they got upstairs, they seemed to load their guns, four, five
or six of them; I hallooed and told them my business, and
requested the man of the house to let the men come down; he
said he would not; three or four made replies, when the old
gentleman called the one (Nelson) by name, and said, "Come
down, Nelson, I know your voice, I know you ;" he said,
"If you come down and go home with me without any trouble
I will look over the past." One of the negroes replied, "If
you take one of us, you must take us over our dead bodies."

The old gentleman then called upon me to go up stairs;
when I attempted to go up, one of the party struck at me with
something that had a prong; I then went out, when they fired
upon the old gentleman and myself ; I then fired, when an ax
was thrown; I told them what the consequence would be in
resisting the law; Parker replied he was a Pennsylvanian,
and did not care for the law; he then asked for them to reflect
and I gave him ten minutes; if he would let me go upstairs
and see if the men were there, I would take them; the warrants were then read; he said there were two men there, but
refused their names; I was told to go ahead, and take them;
advised coolness, and I gave Parker five minutes more to consider; they then counselled upstairs; and asked me to send for
a neighbor; this was objected to by the old gentleman and his
son; old Mr. Gorsuch asked me to call upon Hannang, with
an Indian negro, to assist; I did so, because I saw there was
going to be a desperate fight, as they were loading their guns

in the mean time; Hannang said nothing, and I asked him if he lived in the neighborhood; he replied that it was none of my business; I asked his name, he said I would have to find out ; he said he did not care for any act of Congress, or anything else.

Elijah Lewis then came up, but previously I had shown him my warrant; the blacks stood off with their guns loaded and primed; I called upon him for assistance, and handed him the papers, which he returned, saying the negroes had a right to defend themselves ; Hannang said the same thing; I then looked down the road and saw about thirty negroes coming up with guns, clubs, and something else; said I would withdraw my men if he would not let the negroes fire, and would let them go; he said he had nothing to do with them; I told him (Hannang) that I would hold both Lewis and him responsible; I begged hard, and told the men under me to leave for God's sake, as another party of negroes were coming ; the blacks then howled and rushed upon us; we all fired pretty much at the same time, when the old gentleman fell ; about sixty or seventy negroes were present.

Henry Murr sworn : I live at Cooperville; have known Scarlett for several years; live at the same place, and am a blacksmith; have spoken a few words to him since this occurrence, at the spring near Parker's house; Scarlett did not say anything to me about it; I told Criley I saw Scarlett riding by the shop door; I said so to nobody; have seen Scarlett since it occurred; Scarlett, I told, it was going to be hard times, as regards the killing transaction; I didn't recollect when; yesterday he stopped at my shop; don't mind what I said much; he said he thought it would; did not say to him, nor did he say the negroes were right; expressed no opinion; I said it was not right; don't recollect what he said; he did not tell me he had been to Parker's, neither did he say he had been to the place; we have a heap of talk, as he is often in the shop; can't say what hour it was that morning; it was before seven o'clock

that he was riding towards me; saw two colored men riding
Hood's horses; one had a gun; they rode down the valley
towards Parker's house; the sun was up; have not seen them
since, and don't think I would know them; can't recollect how
soon after I saw three colored men ride by after I saw Scarlett;
neither do I remember which was the first I saw.

Question by J. W. Ashmead : Can you tell the Commissioner whether five minutes or an hour elapsed between the
time when you saw the colored men go by and Scarlett returning; how long do you think it was?

Answer : It may have been fifteen minutes or a little longer.

Henry Kline recalled : I saw William Brown there, and he
was one of the ring-leaders at Parker's; he was there and one
of the most active; he had a gun, and was near the lane; he
was one of the fifteen or sixteen who raised up their guns near
the post.

Miller Thompson, colored, sworn : Lives with Isaac Moore,
father's name is Ezekiel Thompson ; knows Parker's home
where the fuss was; have been often in it; is near a mile from
where we live; William Parker and Pinckney lived in it; was
not there on Thursday, but was at work at Moore's; I heard
about it from Levi Hineman, the carpenter, who had been
thrashing a night or two before, and he allowed he had a
notion to go some place that I forget; saw Jake Wood and
Pete Wood and old John Williams, and Henry Curtis; saw
them coming from the place after it had taken place, ten or
eleven o'clock; I asked them what was going on, and they
told me; they had clubs in their hands; said they had a fight
over there and that a man was killed; they allowed the man's
son got shot or wounded; allowed Pinckney struck his master
over the head with the fence rail; they have all gone off.

George Washington Harvey Scott, recalled and confronted
with William Brown, a Mulatto : I saw Brown at Parker's on
the morning of the murder; he was outside when I saw him,
on last Thursday morning; it was after the horn was blown

from the house of Parker; he was among the colored people then; he was armed with a gun; when I came away I left them all there and Brown among the rest; did not see him fire a gun.

Cross-examined by Brown : Did you see me there George ?

Answer : I saw you there, in the yard, pretty soon in the morning.

Examination resumed direct : Did you see Brown run up the road after the nephew was wounded, with the other colored people?

Here the testimony closed, at about nine o'clock, on Saturday evening, which resulted in the committal of the following named prisoners, to answer the charges of treason against the United States, by levying war against the same, in resisting by force of arms, the execution of the Fugitive Slave law, and also for obstructing the Marshal in the execution of the process of the United States : Joseph Scarlett, white, and William Brown, colored.

It will be noticed that several persons were seriously implicated, some of whom were confined in Lancaster jail, having been arrested on Friday evening. The testimony of Murr was very prevaricating, and he was accordingly held in $500 to appear before the United States Circuit Court, on the first Monday in October to testify.

George Washington Harvey Scott, whose testimony was all important, and was given in a straightforward manner, as was also that of Miller Thompson, a colored boy, were committed as witnesses.

The females were all discharged, and the balance of the colored men detained in custody. Kendig, the white man, was also released.

CHAPTER VI.

THE HEARING RESUMED.

SEVERAL arrests were made at an early hour Sunday morning. The names of the parties were James Hood, white; Ezekiel Thompson, Daniel Caulsberry, Emanuel Smith, John Dobbs, Lewis James Christmas, Elijah Clark, Benjamin Pendergrass, Jonathan Black, Samuel Hanson and Mifflin Flanders, colored. The first two colored persons named were clearly identified as having been participants in the outrage and were fully committed to answer. The excitement was very great. Several hundred persons were present and the deepest feeling was manifested against the perpetrators of the outrage. Although some thirty arrests had been made, a number were discharged, and upon each occasion a certificate to that effect was given them to prevent a second arrest, in case they should encounter any of the officers.

At two o'clock Sunday afternoon, the United States Marshal Mr. Roberts, U. S. District Attorney, J. W. Ashmead, Esq., Commissioner Ingraham, and Recorder Lee, accompanied by the United States Marines, returned to the city. Lieutenant Johnson, and Officers Lewis S. Brest, Samuel Mitchell, Charles McCully, Samuel Neff, Jacob Allbright, Robert McEwen, and ——— Perkenpine, by direction of the United States Marshal, had charge of the following named prisoners, who were safely lodged in Moyamensing prison, accompanied by the marines : Joseph Scarlett, white; William Brown, Ezekiel Thompson, Isaiah Clarkson, Daniel Caulsberry, Benjamin Pendergrass, Elijah Clark, George W. H. Scott, Miller Thompson and Samuel Hanson, all colored. The last were placed in the Moyamensing prison, to await their trial for treason, etc.

The excitement attending the conveying of the prisoners to Moyamensing was tremendous, an immense crowd of people following the officers and marines.   Lieuts. Watson and Jones, who commanded the marines, deserved much credit for the manner in which they performed their duty.

Henry H. Kline recalled :   Ezekiel Thompson was one of the first men on the ground on the morning of the murder; he is the man I designated yesterday as the Indian; he came with Hanway ahead; he went away, was gone a couple of minutes, and returned with a revolver and corn cutter in his hand; he came up to me, and I said, "you —— ——, if you come up to me, I'll blow your brains out ; " he then stepped back a little, and I took my revolver and held it up towards him; his revolver was in his right hand, and the corn cutter in his left; he stood there while I was arguing with Hanway and Lewis, asking them to assist, and reading my paper, I mean the warrants when they asked me to show my authority; Hanway went to twenty or thirty blacks who stood with their guns pointed towards me, and he talked to them in a low voice; after he spoke to them, he moved his horse, and they gave one shout, and moved a little further, he with them, and they fired; another party, some fifteen or twenty, came and presented their guns and fired ; they were about thirty yards off ; I am positive this is the man ; I told him I knew him.   [The prisoner admitted that the witness had told him so.]

Daniel Caulsberry was there, and with the first party ; he came from toward Mr. Rogers, by the creek; he had a gun and a shot bag, or flask, over his shoulder; the party in the house shot at me, and the old gentleman, Gorsuch; they had not been three minutes in the house before they fired; this is the man I mentioned before, with the military whiskers; I have no doubt about him; he was then dressed differently.

Isaac Moore affirmed :   I live at Cooper's factory, about three quarters of a mile from Parker's house; was within hearing, but the threshing machine prevented me; did not know a-half of it until I heard three men were killed; heard about nine o'clock, by a woman who came for peaches; was never near the place till that morning.

Samuel Hanson sworn : I passed Parker's house on the morning of the fight, which was just over; a good many of them were going away; as I was coming down the lane I heard the firing of guns; saw colored people there; a good many of them had arms, guns, etc., but I did not know many; saw Parker; Pinckney I know; saw Isaiah Clarkson there; think I saw Mr. Scarlett there; don't know that I saw Brown; saw Ezekiel Thompson there; did not see Caulsberry; think I saw Peter Wood; saw Jake Woods there; Henry Curtis I saw; saw John Williams there; saw Hanway up the lane on a horse; not Lewis; don't remember any more; after I started these persons came up to me, and talked to me; they talked about the fight; they said the kidnapers ought not to come there; heard one was killed; can't mind what they said.

The persons arrested up to Monday evening, as we find their names, were J. Castner Hanway, Elijah Lewis, Joseph Scarlett, Samuel Kendig, Henry Sims, George Williams, Wilson Jones, Charles Hunter, Francis Harkins, Benjamin Thompson, John Halliday, William Brown (No. 1), William Brown (No. 2), Elizabeth Mosey, John Morgan (boy), Joseph Benn, John Norton, Lewis Smith, George Washington Harvey Scott, Susan Clark, Tamsey Brown, Eliza Brown, Eliza Parker, Hannah Pinckney, Robert Johnson, Miller Thompson, Isaiah Clarkson, and Jonathan Black.

A number of additional arrests had been made since Sunday noon, the result of which was that Henry Green, William Williams, John Halliday, William Brown, (the 2d), George Reed, and Benjamin Johnson, were fully committed to answer. They were taken to Moyamensing prison that evening by Officers Hickman, Stewart, Close, Hand, White, and Butler. Peter Woods, another of the accused, was taken to Lancaster.

Joseph Moore was held in $2000 to answer the charge of

having obstructed the officer in the discharge of his duty.

Charles Smith, a witness, was held to bail in his own recognizance to testify.

A full report of all the testimony is annexed.

Peter Woods (a lad) sworn : I live at Cooperville, near four miles from here; know Jake Woods and Peter Woods; have seen Henry Curtis down here at Kane's; know John Williams; don't know my age; Jake Woods is my brother; know a colored boy named Miller Thompson; don't know where Jake Woods is; I did not see him the day the murder was committed ; he was working at a house of Cooper's, near the scene of the murder, which is about three fields off ; Jacob Moore, John Thomas and William Dorsey were on the fence when I was arrested; I saw none of these at the place the morning of the murder, before they ran they said, " here they all are," when the officers came up; have not seen Curtis since the Quarterly meeting, and don't know where Williams is.

Henry H. Kline recalled : It is my belief that Henry Green is one of the men who was present; he answers the description except that he has plaited his hair since; he was in the first gang.

I arrested William Williams and am positive as to him, can't say now that he had arms ; he was there in the first party that came ; they stood ready with their guns.

John Halliday was there; can't say as to his being armed. He was there in the first party that resisted me; saw him on the ground, and also with those coming back after the fight.

William H. Millhouse sworn : I live right here in the Valley and am in the employ of Philip T. Boone; he sent me to Isaac Walker's on Thursday to repair a threshing machine; when I reached there I did not find my help; on the way I met · a man whom I believed to be the brother of the man who owned the machine, and talked with him, and he asked me why we did not take old Isaac Warner on Saturday; told him I did not know the reason; he said he thought he should be taken, because he saw Squire Chamberlain and him standing in the road talking and after they parted he saw this; saw Warner going to Joseph Moore's; he believed that the negroes had got information through this Squire; about that time these blacks left.

Henry H. Kline recalled : I believe Mr. Brown, (the 2d), was there in the first party, armed, and near the Indian negro.

Thomas T. G. Pearce sworn : It is my impression that William Brown, (the 2d), was there; he resembles the man who shot Gorsuch.

Henry H. Kline recalled : George Reed was there : this fellow and two others came over the field after the first fire; he had the same hat upon his head that he now wears.

Benjamin Johnson was at the ground during the fight, and was one of the ring-leaders; he was in the first party; when they went into the house he was just behind them; he was heated, as if he had ran a great distance and carried a gun.

Henry Young sworn : Wednesday. before the fight I was talking with Dr. Kane; John Clark and Josephus came together down the turnpike near here, about three-fourths of a mile from Christiana; Josephus and Clark came up and entered into conversation with Dr. Kane and me; he (Josephus) presented a paper; he had a gun in one hand and a paper in the other ; he said, "Doctor, can you read the paper to us"? The Doctor tried to read it; could only make out one name, Buley, and Clark said, "I know who that is." The paper was read, and was a notice from Samuel Williams, of Seventh and Lombard streets, Philadelphia. He gave notice that the kidnapers and the Marshal were coming up, and they must be prepared to meet the Marshal, and also to notify the people. Then I went to my work.

John Jackson sworn : I was down in the field when Moore came to us and told me to clear out of the field, and he would go out first, and clear himself (Moore), that the men were coming after us; Henry Morgan, a black, was with me. I understood it to be the officers who were coming to arrest ; he told me that when he blew the horn I must stay away.

Joseph Moore was here confronted with Jackson, and asked if he (Moore) had told him (Jackson) to clear himself?

Jackson replied that Moore said when the horn blew he must clear out.

Samuel F. Mitchel, an officer, sworn : I went to Moore's house to arrest Jackson on Saturday ; saw Moore go in and set down to the table ; he said there were two, one came in and sent him out to the other, Jackson, to tell him to come into his dinner ; he said he had blown the horn for them to come in ; then when I got Jackson, we searched the barn ; we found Jackson in his own house, about half a mile off ; in coming in he made the statement.

Moore declined cross-examining Mitchel, and said : "I said I would go to the house, and know nothing about it."

William Johnson sworn : I heard Charles Smith and Samuel Whitson say, that he, Charles Smith, knew of it the morning before it happened ; they had notice the day before at Penningtonville ; he said so where the old gentleman was lying killed ; Whitson, who is his father, asked him if he would not go over to Levi Pownall's and see the wounded man that was shot.

Maria Russell, white, sworn : John Jackson came home with a club ; he lives on Buck hill, next to me ; it was on Thursday morning, the day of the murder, between 8 and 9 o'clock ; he said that Morgan had shot him first, and that he, Jackson, had struck him on the head with a club, and showed it ; I gave it to the officer, Vanderslice.

Josephus Washington sworn : Know Dr. Kane ; know John Clark, who lives in the house with me ; don't know Williams ; he did not send me a notice that Dr. Kane read to me on the turnpike ; was on the turnpike with Clark ; George Williams had a little piece of paper in his hand, and while sitting on the fence he gave it to me ; I told him I could not read ; I took the paper, put it in my pocket, and afterwards gave it to Dr. Kane to read ; after he had read it he made mention there was no name signed to it, or nothing but three men's names ; one John and Nelson and another ; I did not know the other ; I had a gun in the forenoon, don't believe I had any then ; gave the paper to Mrs. Phillips next morning, and asked her to read it ; she made nothing more out of it than that ; George Williams said he got it from a fine, portly-looking yellow man, who came from Philadelphia ; I hove away the notice after Mrs. Phillips read it.

Charles Smith affirmed : A colored man came to my place the morning Kline came up, and told me they were upon a hunt of slaves ; he said they wanted us to give them information, and let the slaves know they were coming ; one of the slaves was named Nelson ; do not know if I should know the colored man or not ; he was a large yellow man, not a negro ; he said he was coming to Boyd's ; he, Boyd, lives adjoining to me ; did not direct him to Boyd's ; remained at my house not more than fifteen minutes ; did not tell me how he knew ; knew the man in the cars, and they knew him ; do not know how he knew the names ; he told me Kline was one of the men coming up ; did not describe him ; he said he left a paper at Christiana, as I understood him ; the written paper I understood contained the names of the persons sought for ; was at Penningtonville when Kline came in, and heard him speak about two men that were hurt in the woods ; this was after the difficulty ; Kline said he would give $5 for any person to go out and bring them in ; there was a good deal of conversation about it, and waited till the morning line came up ; he said the men were not dead when he left, and that it was a pity they should be left in the woods with no one to take care of them ; I told him that for me, I was willing to go and bring them to Penningtonville ; brought my carriage, and three men went with them in ; the corpse of Mr. Gorsuch was lying in the orchard when we got there ; was a crowd of people there ; do not know these blacks.

At ten o'clock at night the examination was concluded, which resulted in the committal of John Jackson and Thomas Butler (colored) to answer the charge of treason, etc., against the United States.

Josephus Washington, John Clark, colored, and Maria Russell, white, were committed to the Debtors' Apartment of the Moyamensing prison, as witnesses.

The above prisoners were taken to Philadelphia about four o'clock that morning by Lieuts. Johnson and Watkins, and Officers Brisst and Brown.

In consequence of the appearance of Officer Kline, an important witness, at Lancaster, further investigation was postponed until the next Thursday, at nine o'clock A. M.

Altogether, by the civil posse furnished by Marshal Keyser, at the request of the United States Marshal twenty-two arrests had been made, the prisoners all being confined in Moyamensing. The testimony against some of them was very strong.

Some thirty officers remained on duty, using the most active exertions in ferreting out the offenders.

The Philadelphia Ledger of Tuesday of that week said :

"The intelligence received last evening, represents the county for miles and miles around, to be in as much excitement as at any time since the horrible deed was committed. The officers sent there at the instance of the proper authorities made a diligent search in every direction, and secured every person against whom the least suspicion was attached. The police force from this city amounted to about sixty men under the marshalship of Lieut. Ellis. Just as the cars started east in the afternoon, five more prisoners, who were secured at a place called the Welsh Mountains, twelve miles distant, were brought into Christiana. They were placed in custody until such time as a hearing will take place."

CHAPTER VII.

THADDEUS STEVENS SCORES A POINT.

THE KIND of testimony relied upon by the Government and its agents to convict peaceable, orderly, and respectable men of the crime of treason, and so "stop the discussion of Slavery both in and out of Congress," may be learned from the opening of Thaddeus Stevens in the examination of Hanway, Lewis, and others, before an Alderman in Lancaster city. These statements were sustained by the evidence introduced. It was fit that such a case should be upheld by subornation and perjury. They were in keeping with the whole proceedings. Never was a more overbearing and high-handed attempt made by tyrants and cowards to intimidate freemen ; and there never went unhung a gang of more depraved wretches and desperate scoundrels than some of the men employed as "officers of the law" to ravage this county and ransack private houses, in the man-hunt which followed the affray.

The Hon. Thaddeus Stevens observed that the course pursued by the District Attorney made it proper that he should briefly state the testimony which the defense would produce. A great crime—the crime of murder—had been committed in this county. All our citizens equally deplore it. It seemed from the evidence already given, that a citizen from Maryland had been murdered by his own slaves, in the unlawful attempt to secure their freedom. The perpetrators, when ascertained and secured, would receive the punishment due their crimes. The question now was, said he, Who are the guilty parties? No witness had in any way implicated any of the accused now present, except one man—the Marshal, Henry H. Kline—and the boy. Kline stated that Hanway and Lewis were in the road at the mouth of the lane, one hundred yards from Parker's house, and refused to aid in the arrest of the fugitives, declaring that they did not care for the act of Congress which Kline expounded to them. He also swore that the colored persons now arrested were present, aiding the murder. The colored boy (Scott) had sworn that he was present at the murder; had seen Simms shoot Mr. Gorsuch, and also saw Morgan hit him on the head with a corn cutter. He had, likewise, stated that he had seen Hanway walking on foot in the lane, among the colored people, before the firing began; and that he did not return home to Mr. Kerr where he worked until after ten o'clock the next morning.

All the witnesses stated that the murder was perpetrated between six and seven o'clock in the morning. In order to show (continued the learned counsel) what brought Lewis and Hanway (two highly respected citizens) to the place we will show that within the last six months or a year, two colored persons who had long resided in the neighborhood, and had families, with whom they were living, had been kidnaped in the night time, by ruffians, without any pretense or authority, and carried by force into slavery, from whence they had never returned; that one of the victims had been knocked down, wounded in several places, before bound with ropes, and that the trail of the kidnapers was traced towards the Maryland line by the blood which streamed from the wounded man; that two of the perpetrators of those offenses, William Bear and Perry Marsh, were known to be in the neighborhood when the affair occurred—on the 11th of September; that all the good people of the neighborhood were much excited by these outrages; that on the morning of the 11th inst. Hanway and Lewis were informed (after the first firing at the house) that Parker's house was surrounded by kidnapers, who were attempting to capture him. Parker was known to be a free man. They immediately started, without arms to protect him.

When they reached the spot and found that these were

regular officers, with proper authority to arrest slaves, they said they would have nothing to do with it. And being asked to aid in the arrest, they refused, stating that it was impossible, seeing the number of armed blacks present, and advised the Marshal to desist, or blood would be shed. They then retired. Their defiance of law is a bold perfidy of the creature Kline, who alone asserts it. His testimony we will destroy, proving that he has perjured himself in the course of the investigation in more than a dozen instances. He swears positively to the presence of his prisoners; he is particularly positive of John Morgan.

We will prove by unimpeachable testimony, by four white, and three black witnesses, that John Morgan, from Wednesday at five o'clock till Thursday night, was not within three miles of the scene of the action, and he slept on Wednesday night with Henry Cole, at the house of Benjamin Cole, seven miles from Parker's; that he was seen at five o'clock Thursday morning at the Swan Tavern, four miles from Parker's; and seen going to his work at Penningtonville; that he breakfasted with his employer at six o'clock, and remained all day at work in his lumber and coal yard. Simms will be proved in like manner, by five gentlemen of high character, to have been employed from daylight of the day the tragedy was ended until Thursday, at his regular business, from two to three miles distant.

The most wicked perjury will be proven against the boy Scott, by whom suborned we do not now state; certainly by none of the respectable relatives of the deceased; but certainly by some of the worthless agents whom the prosecution have used in the continuance of this unfortunate affair. Harvey Scott lived with Mr. John Kerr, a blacksmith, from three to four miles distant from Parker's; he worked with him as striker and blower; he slept in the garret of a two-story brick house. Mr. Kerr's granddaughter, who had been on a visit to his house for a week or more, slept in a room through which

Scott passed to his garret.   During their stay the door leading to Scott's room has every night been fastened on the outside, and in the morning unfastened, to let Scott out.   On Wednesday night, Mr. Cochran, Mr. Kerr's son-in-law, who lived in the same house, saw Scott go to bed.   Mr. Kerr fastened the door.   In the morning at the break of day, he called Scott to get up.   He answered, came down, brought up the cows, took breakfast, went to the shop, and worked with Mr. Kerr during the whole day.   This will be clearly proven by both Mr. Kerr and Mr. Cochran.   If we prove these facts, nothing will be left to implicate any of the accused but the undoubted perjury of Kline and Scott.   The proof of the absence of the other prisoners will be equally conclusive.

PARKER'S HOUSE, 1897.

CHAPTER VIII.

A WESTERN VIEW.

THE Cleveland True Democrat, speaking of the riot said :
" This is the first horrible tragedy which has taken place
under the Fugitive Slave law.   We had expected such a catastrophe before this; and, we fear, it is but the beginning of a
series of riots which will end, as it has begun, in blood.

" The greater portion of the Democratic press throughout the
country are expressing astonishment and indignation at a slave
shooting his pursuer.   The editors of such papers would do
well to study history and human nature a little.   Liberty is too
sweet, when once tasted by a southern slave, to be lost without
a struggle; and slavery has but poor inducements, indeed, to
offer to such a one, that he would prefer it to death.   'Liberty
or Death !' was the watchword which ran along the lines of
the American army in the Revolution; and are we to look
surprised and stand aghast, when we find our colored brethren
following the example of our forefathers?

" Liberty is as sweet to the negro as it is to the white man;
slavery as bitter.   There is no man so dull as to prefer the
former; and low as the negro race is said to be by pro-slavery
advocates, we do not believe there is a slave, from Mason and
Dixon's line to Florida, who would not undergo hunger, thirst
and severe privations, to realize the glorious boon of freedom.
When a slave escapes, he has made up his mind to undergo
many hardships to reach a land of liberty; and when he finds
himself pursued by slave-hunters, he has but to choose between
slavery and freedom.   Before him is liberty—behind him is
slavery.   And it takes little to encourage him to risk his life
for the former—the latter being but an endless servitude and
degradation.

"The Fugitive Slave law was framed and passed to preserve the Union ; but, we fear it will prove the most disuniting act which Congress has ever passed. Northern men have not that respect for the peculiar institution of the South that they will risk their lives to save it ; and if their homes are to be made the scenes of bloodshed, through the hunting of negroes, the Fugitive Slave law will find fewer supporters. It is one thing to applaud compromises, while they are merely reading them in the newspapers ; and quite another thing to be compelled to prevent slaves from cutting their pursuers' throats.

"But how this case reveals the enormous iniquity of the Fugitive act ! Every attempt to execute it has done that. Every attempt has displayed more vividly its outrage upon humanity and justice. No matter what has been done—whether the avarice of the master has been satisfied by money, whether the law has executed its work, and sent back the fugitive to eternal slavery—this act has been felt more and more to be, as it is, an insult to liberty and a disgrace to the land. But this late development at Christiana, has, beyond all the cases which have occurred, developed its huge enormity. Gorsuch and party counted upon success ; they knew the utter degradation of the negro ; they thought he was like a worm, upon whom they could put their foot at will ; and, standing upon the spirit of those who framed it, and who now seek to carry it out, they violated a right which no King of England would dare do—they broke open a man's house, with intent, by violence, to bind him, and bear him off as a slave. They were killed in the attempt. In their own blood was written the fact, that man can never be so debased as to lose all the attributes of his manhood ; and, instead of whining and writhing over this 'horrible massacre,' let every citizen, worthy the name, turn to the cause of it and have manliness enough to demand the remedy. Let the demand be, the repeal of the Fugitive Slave law, that we may rid our records of a statute fit only to be framed and executed in the bottomless pit, and

our country of inhumanity which will blot over its very name
with infamy, among those, the world over, whose humane
sensibilities are not seared by avarice, or steeled by ambition.''

The Pennsylvania Freeman in viewing the situation put it
in this vigorous way :

'' Have not our press, pulpit and statesmen lauded Kossuth,
Garibaldi, Mazzini and their countrymen as heroes for their
attempt to defend their own rights, and wrench their liberties
from the hands of tyrants by the slaughter of those tyrants?

'' At the same time has not this Nation crushed millions of
its own people under wrongs far heavier than ever drove
Polanders, Hungarians or Italians to bloody resistance? What
wonder they put in practice some of the violent teachings to
which they have listened from childhood? Would it not be
well for those who denounce them as murderers and traitors to
ask themselves whether they would not have defended their
own liberty, and that of their own wives and children, by
similar means?

'' The opinions of the Abolitionists in reference to violent
measures are well known, and by none better than the base
calumniators who charge them with instigating this act of
armed resistance.''

CHAPTER IX.

THE TRIAL FOR TREASON.

THE United States Circuit Court at Philadelphia, Judges Grier and Kane presiding, met on Monday, (November 24) for the purpose of commencing the cases of alleged treason, arising out of the disturbances which took place at Christiana, during the progress of which Mr. Gorsuch was killed and his son badly wounded.

The task of selecting a jury extended over a week, when enough were finally empanelled. The following are their names with the counties of their residence :

Robert Elliott, Perry.

James Wilson, Adams.

Thomas Connelly, Carbon.

Peter Martin, Lancaster.

Robert Smith, Adams.

William R. Sadler, Adams.

James M. Hopkins, Lancaster.

John Jankin, Perry.

Solomon Newman, Pike.

Jonathan Wainwright, Philadelphia.

Ephraim Fenton, Montgomery.

James Cowden, Lancaster.

Peremptorily challenged by defendant : Hugh Ross, Andrew C. Barclay, Robert Ewing, John Clendennin, George G. Bush, Matthias Richards, Marmaduke Moore, William Williamson, James Harper, Moses W. Coolbaugh, Daniel O. Hitner, James Whitehill, William Stevens, John A. Brown, Gen. Cadwallader, Robert Patterson, Patrick Brady, John O. Deshong, George Marks, Diller Luther, James Gowen, Daniel Lyons, John S. Schroeder, Jacob Ketchline.

Challenged for cause : John Rupp, Jonathan Cook, John Smith, J. Lewis, Thomas S. White, Samuel Yohe, John T. Bazeley, Philip Snyder, Hartman Kuhn, Martin Newcomer, Andrew K. Witman, David Cockley, David George.

Set aside by the United States : Lesher Trexler, Sketchly Morton, Joshua Elder, William Watson, Frederick Hipple, Levi Merkle, Paul S. Preston, Edward Davies, Daniel West, George Maderia, William H. Keim, Michael Jenks, James Penny, Ferree Brenton, Franklin Starboard, Isaac Mather, John B. Rutherford, Jacob Grosh, George Sadley, John H. Kinnard.

A number of jurymen applied to be excused on various grounds, mainly because they were hard of hearing. These applications were so numerous that Judge Grier remarked : "It seems as if the whole country is becoming *deaf*—an epidemic, I am afraid, is prevailing."

District Attorney Ashmead stated that he proposed to proceed with the trial of Castner Hanway in the morning.

Judge Grier said that in a case of such importance he did not wish to hurry them ; but he wanted to get through one case in two weeks, so that he could be in Washington by that time.

Thaddeus Stevens, Esq., replied, that one case, he hoped, would be finished in half that time. Up in his county they hang a man in three days, and he trusted that the gentlemen here would not ask for a longer time.

Those challenged for cause (that is, on account of prejudice) were excused from further attendance. Those who were peremptorily challenged and those who were set aside by the Government, were all liable to be called upon to try the other prisoners. These, however, had leave of absence till the next Monday.

Thursday being Thanksgiving, the Court adjourned till Friday morning. The counsel agreed, in order that the jury might not be compelled to pass Thanksgiving with an officer, that the last juryman should not be sworn in till Friday. Judge Kane informed the jury that the Court had engaged a suite of rooms at the American Hotel, where they could take wardrobes and make themselves as comfortable as their situation would warrant.

Judge Grier, while the jury was being empanelled, said that some newspapers had attempted to decide the nature of this offense in advance. The post office has been filled with papers from the Athens of America, as she calls herself, in which this whole case is settled ; for which he did not thank her. If this thing was persisted in he would have to instruct the jury not to look at papers from that quarter.

Mr. Stevens : I hope your honor will direct them not to look at missives from the other quarter.

Judge Grier : Have not seen any.

Mr. Stevens : I have, but they have not convinced me, any more than the others have your honor.

Afterwards the judge repeated his charge to the jurors not to allow anybody to talk with them as to the law or the facts of the case, nor read any papers that attempted to settle the law which governed it, whether they came from the East, West, North or South.

The questions propounded to the jurors by the District Attorney, as they were called, were altered so as to read as follows :

1st. Have you formed or expressed an opinion relative to the matter now to be tried ?

2d. Are you sensible of any prejudice or bias therein as may effect your action as a juror ?

3d. Have you formed an opinion that the law of the United States known as the Fugitive Slave law of 1850, is unconstitutional, so that you cannot for that reason convict a person indicted for a forcible resistance thereto, if the facts alleged in the indictment are proved, and the Court held the statute to be Constitutional?

Of the appearance of the prisoner, The North American
speaks as follows : "The prisoner, yesterday, as on Tuesday,
displayed the greatest self-possession during the selection of
jurors, and the argument consequent upon their rejection or
admission to try him.   He is apparently about 35 years of age,
tall, but spare in form, and inclining to stoop a little.   There
is becoming seriousness in his countenance, but nothing like
alarm or trepidation is visible.   When called upon to look at
the jurors summoned to try him, he does so with a firm and
inquiring look ; but never determines upon his admission or
rejection until he has consulted Thaddeus Stevens, Esq., who
sits immediately at his side.   Upon Mr. Stevens's judgment or
knowledge of the juror he seems to rely implicitly."

CHAPTER X.

SPECIFICATION OF CHARGES.

JOHN W. ASHMEAD, U. S. Attorney General, opened the case for the Government on Friday, November 28, in the following plea : The treason charged against the defendant is, that he wickedly devised and intended to disturb the peace and tranquility of our United States, by preventing the execution of the laws within the same, to wit : A law of the United States, entitled, "An Act respecting fugitives from justice, and persons escaping from the service of their masters, approved February 12, 1837," and also a law of the United States, entitled, "An Act to amend and supplementary to the act entitled 'An Act respecting fugitives from justice, and persons escaping from the service of their masters, approved February 17, 1837,'" which supplementary act was approved the 18th of September, 1850, generally known as the Fugitive Slave law. The overt acts, which may be considered as the evidence or manifestation of the manner in which the treason was committed, are set forth in the indictment as follows :

1st. That on the 11th of September, 1851, in the county of Lancaster, and within the jurisdiction of this Court, the defendant, with a number of persons, armed and arrayed in a warlike manner, with guns, swords, and other weapons, assembled and traitorously combined to oppose and prevent, by intimidation and violence, the execution of the laws of the United States already adverted to, and arrayed himself in a warlike manner against the said United States.

2d. That at the same time and place, the said Castner Hanway assembled with others, with the avowed intention, by force and intimidation, to prevent the execution of the said laws to which I have alluded, and that in pursuance of this combination he unlawfully and traitorously resisted and opposed Henry H. Kline, an officer duly appointed by Edward D. Ingraham, Esq., a Commissioner of the Circuit Court of the United States, from executing lawful process to him directed against certain persons charged before the Commissioner with being persons held to service or labor in the State of Maryland, owing such service and labor to a certain Edward Gorsuch, under the laws of the State of Maryland, who had escaped into the Eastern District of Pennsylvania.

3d. That in further execution of his wicked design, the defendant assembled with certain persons who were armed and arrayed with the design, by means of intimidation and violence, to prevent the execution of the laws already alluded to, and being so assembled, knowingly and wilfully assaulted Henry H. Kline, the officer appointed by the Commissioner to execute his process, and then and there, against the will of the said Henry H. Kline, liberated and took out of his custody persons before that time arrested by him.

4th. That the defendant, in pursuance of his traitorous combination and conspiracy to oppose and prevent the said laws of the United States from being carried into execution, conspired and agreed with others to oppose and prevent by force and intimidation the execution of the said laws, and in the ways already described, did violently resist and oppose them.

5th. That the defendant, in pursuance of his combination to oppose and resist the said laws of the United States, prepared and composed divers books and pamphlets, and maliciously and traitorously distributed them, which books and pamphlets contained incitements and encouragements to induce and persuade persons held to service in any of the United States by the laws thereof, who had escaped into this district, as well as other persons, citizens of this district, to resist and oppose by violence and intimidation the execution of the said laws, and also containing instructions how, and upon what occasions the traitorous purposes should and ought to be carried into effect.

The overt acts which I have now described embrace all the charges which the Government presents against the defendant. I need not say to you that they are altogether of an extraordinary character, and such as, in this country, are but seldom presented for the consideration of a court and jury. In monarchical governments, it is true, crimes of this description are of frequent occurrence, but in a government like ours they are seldom committed. The tyranny to which the subjects of despotisms are exposed may so burden and oppress them that longer submission becomes intolerable, and they are driven to efforts to shake it off. The failure to succeed involves them in the guilt of treason, and trial and conviction for the offense follows as a consequence. I will also state that there are two or three matters which will appear in the course of the testimony to which I shall call your attention.

(*a*). That so soon as Hanway appeared at the bars the negroes at Parker's house evidently appeared to be encouraged and gave a shout of satisfaction, when before that they had appeared discouraged and had asked for time.

(*b*). That before the firing commenced Kline had given orders to his party to retreat and they were actually engaged in the retreat when the attack was made.

(*c*). That Edward Gorsuch, who was killed, had no weapon of any kind in his hands, and was therefore cruelly, wantonly and unnecessarily wounded by the defendant and his associates, while carrying out their combination and conspiracy to resist, oppose and render inoperative and void the acts of Congress referred to in the indictment.

The subject which remains for me to consider is, whether the facts which I expect to prove, amount to such a forcible resistance to the public law, as makes the actors in it guilty of treason in levying war against the United States. I propose now to consider this question, and with that view invite your attention, as well as that of the Court, to a consideration of the law of the case. I need not say that you will receive the law from the Court, and that you are bound by the instructions which the Court may give in respect to it. In this particular there is no difference between civil and criminal cases. It is, therefore, in no sense true, that you are judges of the law, and you must take the interpretation which the Court puts upon it. You have a right to apply the law to the facts, but you have no right to go further. What then is the law? I have stated that treason against the laws of the United States consists, according to the Constitution, only in levying war against the United States, and giving to their enemies aid and comfort. What is meant by levying war against the United States, I proceed now to consider. It is a phrase, the meaning of which is well settled and understood, both in England and the United States. The Statute of 25th Edward III, Chapter 2, contains seven descriptions of treason, and two of them are thus stated by Blackstone :

(a). If a man do levy war against our Lord the King in his realm.

(b). If a man adhere unto the King's enemies in his realm, giving to them aid and comfort in the realm or elsewhere.

These are the two kinds of treason which are defined in the Constitution of the United States, and the words used to describe them are borrowed from the English Statute, and had a well-known legal signification at the time they were used by the framers of the Federal Constitution. This is expressly stated by Chief Justice Marshall, 2 Burr's trial, 401, his language being that "it is reasonable to suppose the term 'levying war' is used in that instrument in the same sense in which it is understood in the English law to have been used in the Statute of 25th Edward III." He then adds that "principles laid down by such writers as Coke, Foster and Blackstone, are not lightly to be rejected." He then defines at page 408, in what levying war consists, viz. : "That where a body of men are assembled for the purpose of making war against the Government, and are in a condition to make war, the assemblage is an act of levying war.'' Coke, Foster, and the other English Elementary writers clearly maintain the doctrine that any resistance to an Act of Parliament by combination and force, to render it inoperative or ineffective, is treason by levying war : and the American authorities adopt the English doctrine. In the cases of the Western Insurgents, 2 Dallas, 345, 347, 355, also reported in Wharton's State Trials, 182, Judge Patterson says : ''If the object of the insurrection was to suppress the Excise office, 'and to prevent the execution of an Act of Congress by force and intimidation,' the offense in legal estimation is high treason ; it is an usurpation of the authority of the Government. It is high treason by levying war.''

Judge Iredell, in the cases of the Northampton Insurgents, in his charge to the Grand Jury, says : ''I am warranted in saying that if in the cases of the insurgents who may come under your consideration, the intention was to prevent by force the execution of an Act of Congress of the United States, altogether, any forcible opposition calculated to carry that intimidation into effect, was a levying war against the United States, and, of course, an act of treason. But if its intention was merely to defeat its operation in a 'particular instance,' or through the agency of a particular officer, from some private or personal motive, though a high offense may have been committed it did not amount to the crime of high treason. The particular motive must, however, be the sole ingredient' in the case, for if committed 'with a general view to obstruct the execution of the Act' the offense must be deemed treason.'' In Fries' case, Wharton's State Trials, 534, Judge Peters in his charge to the Grand Jury, says : ''It is treason in levying war against the United States, for persons who have none but a common interest with their fellow-citizens to oppose or prevent by force, numbers or intimidation, a public and general law of the United States, with intent to prevent its operation, or compel its repeal." Again, "Although but one law be immediately assailed, the treasonable design is completed, and generality of the intent designated by the part assuming the government of the whole. Though punishments are designated by particular laws for certain inferior crimes, which, if prosecuted as substantive offenses, and the sole object of the prosecution, are exclusively liable to the penalties directed by those laws, 'yet when committed with treasonable ingredients' these crimes become only circumstances or overt acts. The intent is the gist of the offense in treason." Judge Iredell, in Fries' case, immediately follows Judge Peters, and referring to the law laid down by Judge Patterson and Peters in the Western Insurgents, 2 Dallas R, 355, says: "As I do not differ from that decision, my opinion is that the same declarations should be made upon the points of law at this time."

Judge Chase on the second trial of Fries, was on the bench, and in an elaborate opinion he maintains the doctrines which had been ruled in the previous cases. Judge Story, in his charge to the Grand Jury, delivered June 15, 1842, 1 Story's Rep., 614, says: "It is not necessary that it should be a direct and positive intention entirely to overthrow the Government. It will be equally treason if the intention is 'by force to prevent the execution of any one or more of the general laws of the United States,' or to resist the exercise of any legitimate authority of the Government in its sovereign capacity. Thus, if there is an assembly of persons with force, with intent to prevent the collection of taxes lawful, or duties levied by the Government, or to destroy all custom-houses, or to resist the administration of justice in the United States, and they proceed to execute their purpose by force, there can be no doubt it would be treason against the United States." Judge King, in his charge to the Grand Jury, on the occasion of the Kensington riots, holds the same doctrine. His language is, that "where the object of a riotous assembly is to prevent by force and violence the execution of any statute, or by force and violence to compel its repeal by the legislative authority, or to deprive any class of the community of the protection afforded by law, as burning down all churches or meeting-houses of a particular sect, under color of reforming public grievance, or to release all prisoners in the public jails and the like, and the rioters proceed to execute by force their pre-determined objects and intents, they are guilty of high treason in levying war.'' To the same effect is the charge of the District Judge, (Hon. John K. Kane) delivered to the grand jury on the 29th of September last. He says, "the expression, levying war, embraces not merely the act of formed or declared war, but any combination forcibly to prevent or oppose the execution or enforcement of a provision of the Constitution, or of a public statute, if accompanied or followed by an act of forcible opposition in pursuance of such combination.''

The authorities and opinions which I have quoted are conclusive of the question of law, and prove that the forcible resistance to the execution of the law of the United States, known as the Fugitive Slave law of 1850, which took place at Christiana on the 11th of September last, in which the defendant participated, with others, if designed to render its provisions inoperative and void, was treason against the United States. It was a levying of war within the meaning of the Constitution. The intent with which the act was committed is the essential ingredient in the offense.

If it was not leveled at the statute, but simply designed to prevent the arrest of slaves belonging to the late Mr. Gorsuch, it amounted, so far as the United States is concerned, to nothing more than a high misdemeanor. The death which resulted from the violence, in this aspect of the case, would be indictable and punishable as murder by the laws of Pennsylvania, but could not be considered an act of treason. It is your peculiar province to pass upon the question of *intent*, and you have a right to infer treasonable designs from the facts and circumstances

which attend the transaction. The combination or conspiracy
of the defendant with others, forcibly to resist the law at
Christiana, can be established without direct proof. "The
concert of purpose," says his honor, Judge Kane, "may be
adduced from the concerted action itself, or it may be inferred
from facts occurring at the time or afterwards as well as before."

In this particular case, however, there is no necessity for
inferential proof, so far as this defendant is concerned. His
resistance to the law was open and declared. He avowed his
determination on the spot, not to regard the provisions of the
Fugitive Slave law of 1850, or any other act of Congress upon
that subject ; and in the very presence of an armed band of
negroes, who had come together to resist the law, he declared
that its supremacy shall not be maintained by him and that the
rights of these insurgents were superior to any statute of the
United States. "They are armed," was his language, "and
can defend themselves."

It is manifest, therefore, that Castner Hanway, so far as in
him lay, had resolved to prevent the execution of these fugitive
slave laws in every instance, and to make them a dead letter
in the neighborhood and county in which he resided, so far as
any ability or influence of his could contribute to that end.
His conduct and language towards Kline incited and encouraged
all that followed afterwards, and the prisoner is legally and
morally responsible for it all. Had he chosen to discountenance
this flagrant violation of law, and held the excited and infuriated blacks in check, the reputation of Pennsylvania would
never have been tarnished by the disgraceful occurrences at
Christiana, and a worthy and respected citizen of an adjoining
state would not have been wantonly and wickedly murdered in
cold blood, while engaged in the assertion of his legal rights.
On Castner Hanway, especially, rests the guilt of the innocent
blood which was spilt on that occasion. He may finally escape
its consequences before this jury, because of some flaw or defect
in our proof, but he can never flee from the reproaches of his

own conscience, or the condemnation which every honorable and upright citizen will pronounce upon his conduct. He is, however, in your hands, and I will say nothing that is in any way calculated to create or array prejudice against him or his case.

CHAPTER XI.

THE EVIDENCE.

G EORGE T. ASHMEAD, for the prosecution, submitted the record of the United States Circuit Court of this circuit, of October 6, 1845, to show that Edward D. Ingraham, Esq., was then appointed a Commissioner by the Court. There being no opposition, the record was admitted and read.

Mr. Ingraham was then called and sworn. He said he had issued that commission (pointing to a paper held by Mr. George T. Ashmead) to Henry H. Kline, appointing him a special officer to execute process for the United States. (The paper was dated March 25th, 1851, and was read.) The witness then said : I also, as Commissioner, issued and gave to Mr. Kline those warrants, pointing to several in Ashmead's hands. (Mr. Ashmead then read the warrants.) They were for the arrest of Noah Bentz, Nelson Ford, Joshua Hammond and George Hammond, alleged fugitive slaves of Edward Gorsuch, of Maryland.

John M. Read, Esq., for the defense, asked that the Court should make an order, before this witness was heard, to exclude the other witnesses from the room during the examination. He wished the witnesses to tell their own stories in their own way.

John W. Ashmead, Esq., said he had no objection to this order, except that some of the friends of the late Mr. Gorsuch were present, and desired to remain.

Judge Grier : The request of the defendant's counsel is a reasonable one, and will be granted. Of course, the order will only apply to those witnesses who are called in regard to the principal facts connected with the affair at Christiana, not to those who may be called for collateral matters. The Marshal will provide accommodations for the witnesses.

Mr. Ashmead : The rule will apply, I suppose, to witnesses on both sides.

Mr. Read : Certainly.

Mr. Lewis : Will our witnesses be excluded now, or when we are about to call them ?

Judge Grier : It might as well be now, but there will be one difficulty in the way here. The newspapers will publish the evidence daily.

Mr. Ashmead : We can't help that, the motion came from the defense.

The witnesses not called then retired, and Henry H. Kline took the stand and was sworn. Mr. Stewart, however; came in at this time and was called and sworn.

Thomas S. Stewart : I am a surveyor ; I proceeded to a house said to be Parker's, at Christiana, and made a survey and draught of it and the roads leading to it ; this is the draught ; all the distances given are correct ; I did not measure the distance from the house to the creek ; I suppose it to be about 1750 feet ; I also made this draught of a house said to be Carr's house ; there are two plans attached to what is called Parker's house, of the upper and lower rooms, partitions and stairways.

The plans were handed up to the judges.

Judge Kane : Are these plans absolute? Did you make the drawing with a camera?

Mr. Stewart : I made the drawings by the rules of perspective ; the trees are correctly placed ; I did not count them, but you will observe I have marked and numbered the rows in the orchard.

The main plan was then exhibited and explained to the jury.

Mr. Ludlow asked the witness why he had marked a certain tree on the plan.

Mr. Lewis objected, as it would lead to mere hearsay testimony from Mr. Stewart.

Mr. Ludlow explained that this tree had been particularly marked at the suggestion of the counsel for the defense, David Paul Brown, Esq.

Judge Grier : Well, what particular harm does it do there ?

Mr. Lewis : The tree ? None, sir.

Judge Grier : Well, then, go on with the case.

Mr. Kline was then called, and papers shown to him. These are warrants placed in my hands on the 9th of September last; I went to execute these warrants ; several persons were to meet me at Penningtonville ; these were Mr. Gorsuch, and his son and nephew, Mr. John Agen and Mr. Tully ; I went to West Chester, and got a horse and vehicle ; we broke down, and I did not meet the persons named at Penningtonville ; I met Samuel Williams at Penningtonville in the morning of the 10th of September ; I went into the tavern and asked about the two horse thieves ; Williams knew me, and said : "Your horse thieves are gone ; you are too late." I started then for the Gap ; Williams followed us about a mile and a-half ; I stopped at the first tavern at the Gap, and called up the landlord ; I inquired for two horse thieves ; the landlord said two men had gone by some time before ; we went to the second tavern, and went to bed ; this was about three o'clock in the morning of the 10th ; we left about 4 o'clock, and went back to Parkesburg ; a man by the name of Gallagher was with me ; we met Agen and Tully at Parkesburg ; they said Mr. Gorsuch had gone to Sadsbury.

About 9 o'clock in the morning I went and saw Mr. Gorsuch. I told him of the accident, and he said he was sorry for it. I told him Agen and Tully were going back to Philadelphia. Agen was constable of the Third Ward, Southwark. I made no arrangement with him ; Mr. Gorsuch had ; so with Mr. Tully. I told Mr. Gorsuch that we had better send the party in different ways, and to prevent Agen and Tully from going, I went down to Downingtown ; saw Agen ; he said he had seen Mr. Gorsuch, and would return to Philadelphia and come up again. About three o'clock, I saw Mr. Gorsuch; he said it was all right. At eleven o'clock at night we walked to Gallagherville; I looked in the cars and could not find Tully and Agen; we then went to the Gap and walked some distance down the railroad, and towards Christiana; about a mile from Christiana we met the guide; old Mr. Gorsuch and the guide walked ahead; we went about a mile and then stopped; Mr. Gorsuch proposed to divide the party; I objected, and said we wanted all and more, too; the guide then took us back through a cornfield; we went on to a creek, where we sat down and ate something; I told them we had better not stop, as it was near daylight; we then went on, I was a little ahead, until we came near Parker's house. (Mr. Ashmead showed a plan here to the witness.) That plan is correct; I know nothing of the others; when we got within forty yards of the house I saw a black man; the moment he saw us he took to his heels, and I after him; this was Josh, or Nelson, I should say; a couple of bars were across the lane; I fell over them; this was in the short lane to the house, as near as I can tell, about fifteen or twenty yards from the long lane; I ran up to the house; Nelson got in before me; old Mr. Gorsuch and another got up a little before me; I went into the house and called upstairs for the landlord; I told him who I was.

Judge Grier: Don't state what was done historically but dramatically. Say what you said then, and what he said, or they said.

Witness: I told them, and said I was an officer and had warrants for Nelson and Josh; they called out there were no such persons there; they then pushed a sharp instrument down stairs at me.

Judge Grier: Was it a pitchfork?

Witness: It was; I don't know what you call it. I then went out and told old Mr. Gorsuch he had better talk to them through the window; one of the blacks then fired, and I fired my revolver; I took out a piece of paper as if to write to the

sheriff for a hundred men ; I did this to intimidate them ; I
read my warrant three times, once in the house and twice out.
I remonstrated with the men ; I spoke to Parker, the landlord,
a colored man. Mr. Hanway then came up to the barn, and
Mr. Gorsuch told me to ask him to help us ; I did so ; I
showed him my warrants ; he read them twice ; I asked him
his name ; he replied it was none of my business ; I asked him
if he lived in the neighborhood, and he made the same reply ;
I told him I had come to arrest Nelson and Josh ; he said he
would not assist me ; that the blacks had a right to defend
themselves ; I asked him if he would speak to them to keep
them off ; he said no, he would not interfere ; there were a
number of blacks in around the house then, with guns, and
were loading them ; the negroes were armed with guns,
scythes, clubs, etc.; a few only were without something ;
Harvey Scott had nothing in his hands ; some fifteen or twenty
negroes came up in the same direction and across the fields
after Mr. Hanway ; one came up immediately after he did,
with a scythe in one hand and a revolver in the other ; a man
named Elijah Lewis came up shortly after Hanway, in his
shirt sleeves ; I showed him my warrant ; he read it and
handed it to Hanway, who read it again and handed it to me ;
Lewis said the blacks had a right to defend themselves, and
that I had better go away, as blood would be spilt ; I saw that
a good many blacks were coming up, and began to beg ; I
asked them to prevent the blacks from firing, and said I would
withdraw my men, but hold them responsible for the slaves ; I
followed Hanway and Lewis up several yards, and begged
them for God's sake not to let the blacks fire and I would
withdraw my men ; Hanway leaned over his horse and said
something to some of the first party ; I did not hear it ; a
short time after I heard them cry out, "He is only a deputy,"
and they fired ; the party number two came up, and when
they saw me they raised to fire, and I went over the fence ;
their shots passed over my head ; I then went back, and saw

Dickinson Gorsuch wounded in the arm; I asked for a doctor, of a man whom I at once recognized to be one of the first in the house; he said there was a doctor at Penningtonville; I saw another man coming up in a hurry on a horse and asked him if he was not one of those who had excited the colored people to this resistance; Lewis and a boy had gone on; I followed them; they went some distance along the road, when Lewis turned off to the right and the boy to the left; I followed up, and saw another boy; I asked him for a doctor, and he pointed to Penningtonville; he said here comes a squire; this man was on a horse; I asked him for a doctor, and he pointed in the same direction; I told him a man had been shot in the woods, and asked if I could get a wagon; he said he did not know; I then started for Penningtonville; I did not know old Mr. Gorsuch was shot then; I met one of my men, wounded and as crazy as a bed-bug; I took him and washed his face at the store; I offered a man a dollar to take us to Penningtonville in his wagon; he took the dollar, but afterwards returned it, and we walked over; when the Lancaster train came up I put the wounded man in it; I waited then some time and offered any one five dollars to go with me to the place; they advised me to remain where I was. I here heard that old Mr. Gorsuch was dead, and his body was brought over for an inquest; there were no witnesses examined; I objected, and said it was a strange proceeding; they made the inquest up themselves, and I gave directions for the disposing of the body; I remained there till next morning, when I started for Christiana; I met Dr. Pearce and told him I was going to look after Mr. Nelson and Mr. Hutchings; I heard that two of my men had been wounded and were in the woods; I met a young man who told me my friends were safe; I saw them afterwards at Lancaster. There were full one hundred negroes at the place, armed as I have stated; when they commenced firing I was a little north of the house and could not see exactly up the lane. I was in the long lane, as far from the short as I am from that gentleman in the jury box ; I had walked there after Mr. Lewis.   [The witness marked the exact spot on the map in pencil, which George L. Ashmead exhibited and explained to the jury.]   Mr. Hanway was forty or fifty yards south, in the long lane, towards the creek, at the time of firing the gun ; this is Mr. Hanway, (pointing to him), I have no doubt ; his horse was stopped, and he was looking back ; several negroes passed him coming to the house ; they passed right by his horse ; one, I think, had a club ; Mr. Hanway spoke to the negro before that ; I did not hear what he said ; after he moved his horse towards the creek they gave a shout and said : "He is only a deputy," and fired ; they were facing Parker's house and me ; I was about as far from them as I am from the opposite wall, about twenty or thirty feet ; the first party did not fire at me ; the second party fired over me about a minute after ; I could not exactly see from where I stood in the corn-field to the bars ; I did not see Edward Gorsuch killed ; I never saw him from the time I left him alive at Christiana until I saw his body.

Judge Grier : What was the effect of the first gun fired from the house and your first fire?

Mr. Kline : Neither took effect ; I fired my revolver straight up to scare them, by letting them know we had arms ; when I met young Gorsuch he was wounded in the arm and body and bleeding from the mouth ; I took him to a tree across the road, on the side with the woods ; he was badly wounded and could not help himself ; I had a conversation with Mr. Hanway about an Act of Congress ; after I showed my warrant I told him as near as I could that the law said, that if any person aided or abetted a fugitive slave in escaping, he was liable to a penalty of $1,000 ; and I think I said to an imprisonment of five years ; he allowed he did not care for any Act of Congress or any other law ; I saw Dr. Pearce and Joshua Gorsuch when I met Dickinson Gorsuch ; they were running down the long lane towards the creek ; they were pursued by a large number of the colored people with guns and other weapons ; I saw Mr. Gorsuch appear to try to get behind Hanway's horse to save himself, or to get on the horse or something or other ; Hanway was going in a trot pretty fast at the time ; when I saw young Dickinson Gorsuch about a mile or a mile and a-half from the scene of action, he was badly wounded and did not know what he was about.

Judge Grier : Is this the person you called one of your men, and said he was "as crazy as a bed-bug ?"

Witness : Yes, sir. The negroes, some of them, wadded their guns in the presence of Hanway ; I saw the colored man, Williams, whom I saw at the tavern at Penningtonville, also at Christiana on the 12th, when the arrests were made ; I saw Lewis there, and said that he was one of the men ; I saw Hanway at Rogers's store the day after the occurrence, and also at Christiana on the day of the arrests ; I recognized him then ; our guide left us before we got to Parker's house ; the old gentleman, Mr. Gorsuch, recognized Nelson and Josh ; I did not know them before ; when we got up there was a good deal of noise in the house ; a horn was blown in the house and several were blown around and about it.

Cross-examined by Hon. Thaddeus Stevens : I think I have before stated that I was told the name of the negro who first saw us at the creek ; I think I said so at my examination at Christiana ; I said then, and I say now, that I chased only one negro, and saw only one ; some of the others saw the second black ; I was a little ahead in running up to the house ; I don't know how those behind me could see more black fellows than I did, except when I fell down ; I don't know where the sound of the horns came from ; don't know that there were echoes from the hills ; I say distinctly that there was no other white man at the mouth of the small lane when Hanway was there ; there was a boy, who came, I think, with Lewis, and stood some distance off ; John Bedley, who was examined at Lancaster, was not there then ; I said at

Lancaster that Scott was there at Christiana, and I say so now. I saw him there with the first party ; he came up with the colored men of the second party when Hanway was there. I am not mistaken ; he had no arms and looked a little scared ; I am positive I got over into the corn-field when I saw them about to pull the trigger on me ; I just got over when they fired ; Dr. Pearce and young Gorsuch appeared to overtake Hanway after he had crossed the creek ; I never told any body I had withdrawn and gone up into the woods before the firing commenced ; I never said I had withdrawn before the firing, commenced that killed Mr. Gorsuch ; there was not a soul said to me at the mill, that I ought to have come away before the firing commenced ; I knew more of the blacks besides Harvey Scott, who were there. I don't recollect their names. I did not name them at Lancaster, I described them. Morgan was there. Henry Sims was there before the firing. George Williams was there. I can't recollect by the name that Nelson Carter was there. I have seen all the prisoners in jail. All that I pointed out were there. I don't recollect Charles Hunter by name.

Mr. Stevens, to the Court : It is necessary that these prisoners now in jail be brought into court. We deem this very essential. We wish to show that the witness has identified most of these people and that his testimony is entirely false.

Mr. Ashmead : There is no objection to this on the part of the government. It is a collateral issue, and the gentleman will be bound by the witnesses' answers. This will save us trouble.

Mr. Stevens : Oh no, this is no collateral matter. It is alleged that war has been levied—we want to see the soldiers. The charge is treason—let us see the traitors. We will go on with the rest of the cross-examination, and ask the Court to send for the prisoners in the morning.

Judge Grier : Very well.

The cross-examination was then resumed by Mr. Lewis. It

was throughout severe and searching, but resulted in the development of no new facts, except what are given. It was very difficult to follow the witness in his examination in chief, as he spoke rapidly, and sometimes indistinctly. He was checked frequently by the Court, the counsel and the reporters, but as he was hard of hearing he seldom halted, and it was as difficult to correct as to report him.

At nearly three o'clock the counsel for the defense held a short consultation, when Mr. Stevens asked the Court for a writ of habeas corpus ad testifiandum for the colored prisoners now in jail. He said it would save time to have them here before this witness left the stand.

Mr. Ashmead : Will not the gentlemen include the white prisoners in their request ?

Mr. Stevens : We have nothing to say of them.

Mr. Ashmead : It would be better to send for all at once.

Mr. Stevens : The gentleman will permit us to judge what we consider best for the defense. He will do the same for the government.

Judge Grier to Mr. Ashmead : You can apply for a writ if you think proper.

Mr. Ashmead : Well, sir, I will then ask the clerk to include in another writ the names of the prisoners not embraced in the defendant's.

Judge Grier : Let a writ be issued, and adjourn the Court until tomorrow, at 10 o'clock.

The object that first struck the eye on entering the Court room on Saturday morning, was a row of colored men seated on the north side of the room. They were cleanly in their appearance, and their heads and faces presented strong presumptive evidence that they had just escaped from the hands of the barber. These were the colored persons alleged to have been engaged in the treason at Christiana, and numbered twenty-four. They were all similarly attired, wearing around their necks " red, white and blue " scarfs. Lucretia Mott was at their head. This, we believe, was her first appearance in Court since the trials had commenced. Her dignified and benevolent countenance ever attracted attention. Under that calm exterior there glowed a fire, kindled by charity, which was as universal as it was ardent and enduring. During the entire session, she sat knitting, apparently unconscious of what was transpiring around her, except when some expression of the witness on the stand was likely to bear strongly against the prisoners. Her eyes would then be raised from her work, and sparkle with animation for a moment, only to relapse into their accustomed quiet and peaceful, but intelligent aspect.

On the opening of the Court that morning, John M. Read, Esq., for the defendant, stated that the cell in which the defendant was confined was too close and badly ventilated and was injurious to the health of the defendant. He was in very delicate health, he said, and asked that the Marshal be directed to furnish a more commodious room.

Judge Grier : As a general rule, the Court would not interfere in such a matter, but we have no objection to do so in this case, in consideration of the health of the prisoner. The Marshal will therefore provide as convenient a place, consistently with the safe-keeping of the defendant, as he can, for his detention.

Mr. Read stated that a large number of witnesses had been called by the defense, and others would be sent for, to sustain the objection pointed out previously in Kline's testimony. The defense was under the impression that the United States would have directed the attention of the witness to the identity of the other prisoners said to have been present at the affair at Christiana, but the prosecution had not done so.

Mr. Read wished to know now, whether the defense would be permitted to ask the witness, Kline, to name and identify the prisoners present, and then to show by other witnesses that those persons were not there.

Mr. Stevens said they wished to ask the witness to name the persons present, and then to contradict him.

Mr. Cooper, for the United States, said the prosecution had not asked the witness any questions in relation to the other prisoners, and did not wish to do so.

Judge Grier said the Court could not interfere with the ordinary rules of evidence, and permit collateral issues of this sort to be raised out of the usual order and rule. The government had not examined the witness on the matters referred to, and the defense were bound by his answers to their questions, as it was clearly new matter.

Judge Kane concurred entirely in the views of Judge Grier.

The counsel in the defense then held a short consultation, at the end of which Mr. Stevens said they had called for the colored prisoners with the view to ask the witness if they were there, at Christiana, and to contradict him if he said they were, but under the ruling of the Court, they would be now withdrawn.

John W. Ashmead said that under the circumstances the white prisoners would be also withdrawn.

Judge Grier : You do not wish to try thirty-eight issues in one ?

Mr. Ashmead : No, sir.

Judge Grier : Let the other witnesses withdraw then, and the trial proceed.

The prisoners were then taken out of the Court, and Mr. Stevens called the attention of the Court to an error in the official report, in which the witness is said to have stated that "after he *resisted*, I told him what the Act of Congress said." This should have been, "after he *refused*," etc.

Judge Kane said the witness spoke so indistinctly, he had supposed, as the reporter did, that he said "resisted."

Mr. Stevens : We all agree, sir. The witness said "refused." Other errors were then pointed out and corrected in the report.

Henry H. Kline was then recalled to the stand and his cross-examination resumed by Mr. Stevens. He said : I never told any one I saw a man shoot old Mr. Gorsuch ; I never said I saw Parker shoot him ; I never said to Jacob Whitson or any-body else that I saw Parker shoot him ; I never told Samuel H. Loughlin I heard Hanway encourage the negroes ; I never told Loughlin that I was up in the woods when the firing in the lane took place ; the firing occurred between three and five o'clock ; can't say any nearer ; I had no watch ; the sun was not up when I read the warrants ; it might have been three quarters of an hour between the time when I chased the negroes up from the creek, to the time when the firing took place ; I did not tell Mr. Cooper or any one else that if my men had stood by me there would have been no trouble, not at all sir ; Cooper walked alongside of me and wanted to talk, but I would not talk with him ; it was on the morning of the 12th ; I had no conversation with him from first to last, good or bad ; I don't know that he was present when I conversed with any one else ; I was very careful of him and what I said ; I did not know Whitson by name ; I recollect going to a man's house on Sunday—if that was Whitson's, I saw a young man there ; I had no conversation with him or any one else there ; the white men at Christiana had no arms that I saw ; six of our party had four revolvers among them ; I don't know who the guide was ; he was a colored man and disguised ; after the fight begun I did not discharge my revolver ; it was about half-past one o'clock when we left the Gap to go to Parker's house ; we arrived at the creek at daybreak.

Re-examined by George L. Ashmead, for the United States : Why were you careful of your conversation with Mr. Cooper ?

Mr. Stevens : I object to that question, unless it is shown that we had something to do with his caution.

Mr. Ashmead pressed the question.

Judge Grier : I don't think it has anything to do with the case. It was very good caution, whoever gave it.

Mr. Brent : Did you see Cooper when the inquest was held on old Mr. Gorsuch's body ?

Witness : Yes, he was there ; he was on the Coroner's jury.

Mr. Lee : What was it you said about Scarlett ?

Witness : The person I saw on a horse, sweating very much, was Scarlett ; he came up after the firing ; he was not there before.

Thomas Pearce, called by the United States, affirmed—examined by George L. Ashmead : I am a resident of Maryland ; I lived near Edward Gorsuch, and am a nephew of his ; I accompanied him, Mr. Kline and others to Christiana on the morning of September 11th, last ; as we passed from Christiana to Parker's we heard a bugle on our right ; the road runs there nearly west ; it appeared to be not very remote, perhaps a quarter of a mile ; it was about daylight when we arrived there ; a black man was seen near the creek, who ran up to the house ; Mr. Kline was a little ahead ; Edward Gorsuch was next, and Dickinson Gorsuch and myself were last ; the first of our party got up as soon as the black, nearly ; when I got up I received a missile from the house ; I have the mark yet ; Kline and the old Mr. Gorsuch got into the house ; there was confusion and noise for some time, and we could not get in ; after some time the warrants for Nelson and Josh were read to the proprietor of the house ; they were read again to him on the outside of the house, when Kline and Gorsuch came out ; the parley was kept up for some time ; the Marshal said he come to arrest the men, and he would not go away without them ; he wrote an order for a hundred men ; the men upstairs asked for time ; the prisoner before me come up to the bars then ; the Marshal read his warrants to him ; the man said to the Marshal, "You had better go home—you can make no arrests here," and said something about blood ; during this time a number of blacks came up armed, while the Marshal stood with the men at the bars ; the Marshal told him and the other (I believe it was Lewis and Hanway), he would hold them responsible for the slaves ; the negroes were then coming up pretty fast, and the Marshal said we had better withdraw, as all the men were armed with guns, corn cutters, pistols or

clubs ; I then went to tell my uncle what the Marshal had
said ; he was returning to the house and was in considerable
danger ; I wished to get our party together ; as I was passing
up I saw one of his slaves in the act of shooting, but cannot
say he fired ; my uncle received the first blow on the head, and
was shot as he fell ; I supposed he was dead ; I got as near to
him as I could for the crowd ; Dickinson Gorsuch got up as
near his father as he could, and found his pistol ; he raised his
pistol a second time, when he was struck ; at this time I passed
out of the crowd toward the bars to escape ; eight or ten shots
were fired before I got over the bars ; I saw Hanway beyond
the bars, looking where my uncle was shot ; I did not overtake
him till he got over the creek ; I asked him to repel the attack ;
Joshua Gorsuch asked him to lend him his horse, or repress
the outrages ; he said he could do nothing for us, and rode off
as fast as he could ; before he came up the negroes were inclined to give up, but as soon as they saw him they seemed
encouraged and determined to repel us ; they gave a yell when
they saw him ; I recognized Bewley, one of Mr. Gorsuch's
slaves, as he ran by me ; I was wounded, as I said, over my
eye ; I also received a shot in my wrist, and two in my shoulder
near my spine ; I saw a negro at the bars with a revolver, but
did not see him fire ; my clothes were also shot, and one ball
passed through my hat, near my head ; the first gun fired, was
fired from the window at my uncle ; the man kept himself behind the window, and therefore did not hit my uncle ; the
negroes who came up when the Marshal and Hanway were
talking at the bars were near enough to hear what was said.
(The witness here explained his position near the bars, by the
map.) I should suppose, at the lowest estimate, there were
eighty negroes there ; I saw several white men running over
the fields, in my flight to the bars ; I did not see Dickinson
Gorsuch after that, until 4 o'clock that evening at Pownall's ;
he was much prostrated ; the doctor said there were about
seventy shot (squirrel shot) in his side and arm ; my opinion

was then, that he certainly must die ; I can't say how long it
was before he reached his home in Maryland ; it was some
three or four weeks ; I saw Joshua Gorsuch the next Saturday
in bed ; his wound was in the back of the head, about three
inches long, and across the suture of his head ; it had a decided effect on his mind ; he talked more and was more easily
excited than before ; it was a wound from a blow with a gun ;
I saw the negro strike at him and saw him fall forward ; after
Hanway left us we run up the lane and they all fired at us ; I
was ahead, and when I looked back I saw the fellow strike
Joshua, as I stated, with a gun I think ; I think I have stated
all the conversation between the Marshal and Hanway at the
bars ; I had some conversation with him myself, but don't
recollect what I said ; I said substantially that I thought his
presence there inspired the negroes.

Question : What was his manner in that conversation ?

Mr. Stevens : I object to that. Let us hear what was said
and done, but don't make the witness a judge of the manners
of those of whom he speaks.

Judge Grier : Certainly, let the witness state what was said
and done.

Witness : The conversation was a decidedly angry one on
both sides.

To Mr. Cooper : The negroes came in parties, and were
generally armed ; one party came by the bars ; Dickinson Gorsuch had his reason when I saw him at Pownall's ; the shout
was given by the party from the house, when the other party
came up ; the firing commenced immediately after my uncle
was knocked down.

To Mr. Brent : The Marshal wrote the order for the one
hundred men, and gave it to Joshua Gorsuch ; I think the
negroes in the house could see him write ; I heard horns before
Hanway came up ; I heard a voice in the house also ; I was
nearer the house when the conversation took place between the
Marshal and Hanway ; the white men I saw appeared to have

come from the creek ; I saw several negroes come up on horses; I saw them load their guns ; Noah Bewley came up with those on horses, but I don't know that he came on a horse.

Cross-examined by Mr. Stevens : I think Mr. Lewis was there when the Marshal and Hanway had the conversation ; I can't say that they were exactly at the mouth of the short lane ; they appeared to be between the bars and the long lane ; I took the colored persons loading their guns to be on the other side of the long lane from where I stood ; I took Kline to be a Marshal or Deputy Marshal ; when I overtook Hanway coming away, he was about midway between the mouth of the short lane and the creek, looking towards the house ; when I went up to look for Kline, the party I saw loading their guns had passed up towards the house to meet those from the house ; there was no firing until the parties met ; I heard no firing in the long lane ; my attention was directed to where my uncle was shot ; I never said that I thought Hanway turned around to stop the negroes ; I stated that my opinion was that he turned back and spoke to the negroes to turn them back. I said I did not know but he might have turned them back, and that I might attribute my safety to that. I never told anyone that I owed my life to Hanway's turning back to speak to the negroes. I gave it as my opinion. I did not tell this to Squire Dickson. I don't know him. I did not say to Doctor Patterson that Hanway turned back the negroes and thereby saved my life. I have stated it as my opinion. (Very positively.) No sir, I never told anyone that Kline was a coward, and that if he had not ran away there would not have been any firing or mischief. I never said this to Mr. Henderson or Dr. Patterson. I said that Kline might have behaved more prudently and kept us together. I did say I thought my uncle had been imprudent in going into the fight. No, I never said to Lewis Cooper that the marshal was a poor thing and ran at the first intimation of danger.

By Mr. Reed : Did you not say the day after the occurrence,

at Pownall's house, to Mr. Cooper or in his presence, that Kline was a monstrous poor thing, and ran at the first intimation of danger?

Witness: I did not, sir.

Re-examined by Mr. Brent: I said that the party nearest to me in my escape continued the pursuit, but that those behind might have been turned back by Hanway. I said that the turning back of these, the main body, might have caused the others to turn back, and therefore saved me. This is what I meant to convey.

Question: Could Mr. Hanway have restrained the negroes if he had tried to do so?

Mr. Stevens objected to this question. What did he say or do, is the proper inquiry.

Mr. Brent: Very well. I will ask then, What did Hanway say or do in relation to restraining the negroes?

Mr. Lewis objected to this question. The witness has said he did not hear him say anything.

Mr. Read: The true difficulty here is, that this is a re-examination in chief, and the question relates to no new matter brought out by the cross-examination. If we are to cross-examine again on the same matter much time will be unnecessarily consumed.

Judge Kane said he thought the question related to matter brought out by the cross-examination.

Witness: I did not hear the defendant say anything to restrain the negroes. I did not hear him say anything on the subject.

To Mr. Cooper: I meant to say that my uncle went back to the fight. I did not mean to say he went back to fight. He had no weapons.

To Mr. Stevens: I did not see that Hanway had any arms.

Joshua Gorsuch, affirmed for the United States and examined by George L. Ashmead, Esq.: I was a neighbor of Edward Gorsuch; I occupy the adjoining farm and am a

cousin of his ; I accompanied him and the others to Parker's
house in September last ; I heard the sound of bugles some
ten minutes before we got there ; they appeared to be at my
right as we went up ; we went on then to the bars that lead to
Parker's house ; we heard some one singing ; some one said
here they are, and jumped over the bars ; when I got to the
house Edward Gorsuch called to his servant, Nelson, to come
down and give himself up, for it would be better for him ; he
said he had seen him ; they said he was not there ; I was then
struck on the shoulder with a piece of wood and heard Dr.
Pearce say he was struck ; I then saw the fire from the window;
Edward Gorsuch said, "You have shot at me ; I demand my
property ;" there was a good deal of conversation ; they said
there were no such persons there ; I said perhaps they had
fictitious names ; the Marshal was then called upon to read his
warrant ; during this time a man rode up to the bars ; I told
the Marshal of it, and he went to speak to him ; the Marshal
called me over to him ; parties of negroes were there, coming
up, and the Marshal said, "Go tell your cousin to come away,
as I will hold this man (Hanway) responsible for his property,
if he is worth it ;" I went to my cousin and told him what the
Marshal had said ; at this time a man came up and struck my
cousin ; I was also struck, and fired at the man to save my
cousin ; I turned to run and was struck again ; I ran down
and met Dickinson Gorsuch and told him I did not expect to
see his father alive again ; I ran down the long lane and saw
the lane filled with black persons and some white men to the
left ; as I ran, every man who could get a lick at me, struck
me ; I overtook a man on a horse and asked him to let me up
on his horse ; I said to the black men, for God's sake don't
kill ; I got to a house belonging to a man named Rogers ; I
did not like his looks, and ran to the woods ; I met the Marshal, Kline, and went on to the store and bought myself a hat ;
I asked some of them to carry me on to Penningtonville ; a man
then said he would take me for a dollar ; I gave him the

money, but he returned it and said he could not take us ; I then went to Penningtonville and took the cars for Columbia ; I arrived at Columbia about 11 o'clock ; I knew the conductor of the cars ; he wanted me to go to Maryland ; I told him I could take no definite information home ; I did not wish to go ; I told him not to inform my family that I was wounded, and he did not until it was reported I was killed ; I saw Joshua Hammond, one of Edward Gorsuch's slaves, at Parker's house ; Joshua was perfectly furious ; I saw another that I took to be Nelson, but would not swear to him ; I am positive as to Joshua ; I heard horns blown before we got there ; the horn blown from the window was blown several times before the negroes came upon the ground ; they told us then there were five negroes in the house ; I don't know of my own knowledge how many there were ; I estimated as near as I could come to it that there were one hundred and fifty negroes there altogether ; I saw one armed with a stone, some with scythes, corn-cutters and clubs ; there might have been guns, but I did not notice them ; I heard no firing until after they commenced murdering Mr. Gorsuch ; I would not have known my mind was affected had I not told the Marshal that I was about five miles from home, and would go to Baltimore ; I was perfectly bewildered and did not know what road to take ; I was as near to Edward Gorsuch when he was knocked down as I am now to Mr. Lee (very near him); I did not notice the man on the horse in the lane as I was running away ; I can't say whether I was fired at as I run away, except what others have told me ; I did not hear the conversation between Kline and Hanway ; I was half way up the lane when Kline told me to carry the message to Edward Gorsuch; I thought the people in the house seemed like dying (or crying) when Kline made a sham to send me for a hundred men; I thought there was no use in that, and said it would only make them worse; when the man came up to the bars, the negroes seemed to take courage; their countenances even lightened up—

Mr. Stevens : I object to that, unless they were white men. [A laugh.]

Witness : They gave a shout, then ; I am yet seriously affected by the injuries I received then.

There was no cross-examination of this witness.

Dickinson R. Gorsuch sworn for the United States, and examined by George L. Ashmead : I am a son of Edward Gorsuch; I accompanied him on the 11th day of September last to Parker's house, near Christiana; I heard a horn blown about half an hour before I got there; as we got near the house I saw a negro come into the lane; I heard my father call out, catch him ! Dr. Pearce and I ran after him; he got into the house first and the negroes ran up stairs; I heard my father calling in front of the house, and went round; I heard the gun fired at my father; the negroes asked for time; I saw a man come up to the bars, and the Marshal said go and summon him; some of them did so, and my father and myself were left at the house; the negroes seemed inclined to give up; I walked towards the bars and saw the man on the horse reading the papers—the warrants; the men up stairs then stamped and shouted, and Parker said, "There he is, take him," meaning Walker, who came up with a gun on a horse, and whom I saw; I saw them go near my father, and went back and raised my revolver; I told my father it was no use, they would kill us all; he said it would not do to give it up in that way; I was then struck on the arm and wounded in the side; I fell against the fence, I suppose; I got up and went over to the other side of the lane ; I was bleeding very much and faint ; I asked a man several times to get me water, which he at last did ; this man I recognized in prison to be Scarlett ; I laid three weeks and a day at Pownall's before I could get home ; when the man came to the bars, the negroes up stairs put their heads out of the windows and said, "There he is ! " they did not say who it was ; I looked at him well enough to distinguish him ; the prisoner, Hanway, is the man ; I had about eighty grains of shot in my body altogether ; I heard a horn blown after we got up to the house.

To Mr. Brent: I passed blood from my mouth before I got the water ; I threw up coagulated blood afterwards ; I did not see Nelson there ; the change in the conduct of the negroes occurred shortly after Mr. Hanway came up to the bars ; I did not hear the conversation. No cross-examination.

Nicholas Hutchings sworn for the United States and examined by George L. Ashmead: I was a neighbor of Edward Gorsuch, in Maryland ; I accompanied him on the morning of September 11 last, to the house of Parker ; I heard a horn blowing as we went there ; the sound came from our right ; when we came to the house Kline told them he was an officer and came to make an arrest ; Mr. Gorsuch heard of his slave upstairs, and told him to come down and he would forgive him ; something was then thrown down, and hit Dr. Pearce ; a gun was then fired out of the window ; Kline read his warrants several times ; a short time after a horn was blown out of the house ; the negroes asked for time to consider ; it was given, and in the meanwhile some man rode up to the bars ; Kline went up to him and asked him to assist ; he showed his warrants, which the man read, and made a reply, which I did not hear ; another man came up, who also read his warrants ; about this time some twenty to thirty negroes came up, armed with scythes and clubs ; Kline called on us to leave, as he would hold these men responsible for the slaves ; we went down the short lane and Kline told us to follow the man Lewis ; I soon after saw Dickinson Gorsuch, bleeding very much, and I made my escape ; I saw the man at the bars go down the lane on horseback ; I did not see his face ; there were one hundred and fifty or more negroes armed with guns, scythes and clubs ; the first gun was fired from the house, over old Mr. Gorsuch ; the negroes in the lane, where the man was at the bars, were loading their guns ; I was certain I saw Noah Bewley, a slave of Mr. Gorsuch, there ; I first saw him and

Dickinson Gorsuch together in the woods ; the negroes were in good spirits when the man came to the bars ; they shouted and hallooed to them ; they were depressed before that.

Cross-examined by Mr. Stevens : I did not see the white men speak to the negroes there ; I saw the man at the bars going down the lane ; his back was towards me.

Nathan Nelson, sworn for the United States : I was a neighbor of Mr. Gorsuch, and accompanied him to Parker's house in September last ; I heard a horn as we got near the house ; we stopped to take something to eat, and saw a couple of negroes come into the house ; we got up to the house, when a club was thrown from the house and struck Dr. Pearce ; a gun was also fired at Mr. Gorsuch and another club was thrown out ; before this, the Marshal had read his warrants ; the negroes asked for time, and some ten or fifteen minutes were given them ; a man came up to the bars on horseback and the negroes gave a shout ; about this time a party of negroes came into the long lane and stood there loading their guns, and picking their flints ; at this time the Marshal called to us to retire, that he would hold these men responsible for the slaves; I walked some distance, when Hanway told us we could do nothing ; I said I thought not ; the last I saw was when the negroes were running Dickinson Gorsuch and Dr. Pearce ; I saw the face of the man at the bars ; I take the prisoner at the bar to be the man ; I had no conversation with him, but when he said we could do nothing, and I said I thought so too ; I heard the firing going on ; I should suppose there were seventy-five or one hundred negroes there ; I heard a horn blown from the house, and others blown in the neighborhood afterwards ; I thought it was an early hour for breakfast ; I can't say that Kline handed Hanway any papers.

Cross-examined by Mr. Stevens : The horn was first blown when we got to the long lane ; we were at the house about an hour ; I can't say exactly where the other horns were blown in the neighborhood ; one came from towards the railroad ; I don't know where Rogers's house is ; I don't know whether it was before or after six o'clock when the horn was blown, but I thought it was early for breakfast ; Hanway was not standing in the long lane, it was at the mouth of the short lane ; there was another man or boy there, named, I believe, John Bedly ; Kline was then some distance off ; I did not see him with Hanway and Bedly ; Hutchings and Kline were ahead of me ; well, I did not say where Hutchings and Kline were before the firing ; I said Hutchings and I were near the woods ; I did not say Kline was there ; the first time I saw Kline and Dickinson Gorsuch, after the firing, was in the woods ; I did not see Mr. Lewis at all ; I don't recollect seeing him ; when Hanway was reading the warrants I did not see Lewis.

Miller Knott, sworn for the United States, and examined by George L. Ashmead : I reside in Sadsbury township, Lancaster county ; have lived there about eleven years ; it is about two miles from Christiana ; I recollect the occurrence there on September 11th, last ; I visited the battle ground that morning some few minutes after the firing ; Mr. Gorsuch was not then quite dead; I saw between seventy-five and one hundred negroes there ; a quantity of them were armed ; I heard a good deal of firing ; I was about two hundred yards from Parker's house when it commenced ; I saw Joseph Scarlett, a white man, there ; I have known him six or seven years, probably longer ; he lives about one and a-half miles from there ; he was on horseback.

Question : Was his horse sweating ? Mr. Read objected.

Judge Grier : Let the man tell his own story, and ask for anything he may omit.

Mr. Ashmead : Well, perhaps, it would be best to turn him over to the defense.

Mr. Stevens : If you turn him over to us, we will turn him out of Court. You can go.

The witness retired, but was recalled by Judge Grier, to know what became of Mr. Gorsuch.

Witness said : We took care of him, and when he died we held an inquest on him at Christiana ; I was not with him all the time ; I went to look after Dickinson Gorsuch, who was wounded.

Mr. Stevens : Did you hear any horns blown from that neighborhood?

Witness : I did not hear any myself.

Mr. Stevens : Well, I only ask for what you heard yourself. You can go now.

John Knott, a little boy, sworn for the United States, and examined by George L. Ashmead : I recollect the battle on the morning of the 11th of September, last ; the firing commenced about sun-up ; there was a good deal of firing ; I saw it from above Parker's house, at about six or seven hundred yards distance ; there were about one hundred negroes there ; I saw a young man who was wounded, up by an oak tree, forty or fifty yards from the short lane ; Kline was with him ; he brought him out and set him down there.

Cross-examined by Mr. Stevens : He was opposite the mouth of the long lane when I first saw him, some forty or fifty yards from the mouth of the short lane. [The exact distance by the map is seventy-one yards.]

George L. Ashmead here stated that there were some ten witnesses yet to be examined for the United States who had not been called to attend today, as it was supposed that those who have been examined would have occupied a longer time. It was near the hour of adjournment, and he hoped the Court would now adjourn.

The Court was thereupon adjourned.

Thaddeus Stevens remarked to Judge Grier that two of the counsel, himself and Mr. Cooper, necessarily would be absent on Monday next, and would "pair off" for the opening of Congress on that day. He said there was important business for that day—the election of a Speaker in the House, and he supposed Mr. Forney was particularly anxious for him to be present also.   There was a hearty laugh at this joke.   Mr. Forney was a candidate on the Democratic side, for Clerk of the House.   Mr. Stevens was a Whig member.

The Pennsylvania Freeman in its issue of that week says : "We can only say that, in our judgment, (and such, we believe, is the almost if not quite universal opinion of those who have watched the progress of the trial,) the Counsel for the Government have not only failed to substantiate the charge of treason, even under their own absurd definition of that offense, but to show that the prisoner was guilty (?) of any other violation of the law than that involved in a refusal to aid Kline and his party in arresting fugitives.   There was some pretty hard swearing on the part of the Government witnesses, but the evidence in behalf of the defense will bring out enough of the truth to secure a prompt acquittal.   We do not believe that any intelligent person anticipates the possibility of any other verdict than one of 'not guilty.' "

CHAPTER XII.

THE TRIAL.—CONTINUED.

THE CASE of Castner Hanway was resumed on Monday morning. The trial had lost none of its interest. The Court-room was again filled, and the usual concourse of people gathered in the passage-ways leading thereto. ·The number of ladies present exceeded that of any previous day, many of whom belonged to the Society of Friends.

David Paul Brown said that he had a suggestion to make to the Court. He stated that a defendant in these cases is confined under the charge, and is in a dying state. He wished his condition might be alleviated. It was probable he would not survive the trials.

The Court directed the Marshal to see that he was properly cared for. His name was Collister Wilson.

Mr. Brown said that he believed others were suffering, among whom was a Jacob Moore, one of the defendants.

Miller Knott sworn: I was aroused on the morning of the 5th by some sharp hallooing; I studied for a moment, when my little boy ran away, and I went after him for fear he would get hurt; my son got there first; it was a little after sunrise when I got there; I saw a man on horseback going away; he was riding towards the north; he had not got to the branch when I saw him; negroes were behind him; I think he had no coat on; if he had it was black; I saw no white men there; there were about fifty blacks between me and the man on horseback; about twelve or fifteen negroes advanced towards where Dickinson was, under the tree; an old colored man came up; I stopped him and said, what is this you have been doing this morning; he said, I have been doing nothing; he said to me, didn't you hear the horn blow; he started to where Dickinson was; I said stop, I want to know more about it; then twelve negroes came up to Dickinson, and I said they will kill him; and I said, save him, save him; he did not answer; then I said, mind what is before you; he then threw up his arms, and turned around, and the blacks went back; they went towards the corn-field, then went into the house; Josiah Clarkson, the colored man got on something high and cried, order! order! and they all became still and quiet. At the time I saw Mr. Gorsuch, was when the blacks were running through the cornfield; he was lying nearer the bars than the house; he was not quite dead then, when I went up to him; no one offered to move him; I saw Scarlett ride in at the mouth of the long lane; his horse was a little sweaty; he rode down the lane towards Parker's house, and then rode out again; I don't know where he went then; I think to the mill; the way that Mr. Hanway would come by the road to the mill would not be a mile; it would be something less by the corn-fields; the firing was over when I got there; Lewis lives about a mile from Parker's house; Scarlett lives about the same distance.

Question by J. W. Ashmead: What was the color of the horse?

Witness: I don't know the color of the horse.

Question by J. M. Read: Where were you at that time?

Witness: I was near the mouth of the long lane at the time, on the road running down towards my house.

John Knott, recalled: I got to this place about ten minutes before my father; I went by the side of the road; standing against the fence I could see Parker's house; they broke out of the house; a little after they came out they fired and dispersed out of the big lane to the little lane; at one time they fired at a tremendous rate; there were about sixty or seventy outside before they broke out; some were at the mouth of the little lane, and some at the bars ; I did not see any white men running ; I did not see any negroes come up on horseback ; I saw three or four horses hitched along the fence in the big lane; I do not know whose horses they were ; I saw one of Mr. Gorsuch's slaves, as they are called, before the light ; he was called John Bier ; the last I saw him was at the brick kiln, about two months before, at Hanway's ; he was passing by at the time ; I did not see any blacks in the light when I saw Dickinson Gorsuch bleeding very much ; he was about five feet from the place where he was seated ; I got some water for him; I held an umbrella over his head ; the negroes came up in a great fury with clubs ; my father said they will kill him ; old Isaiah Clarkson, he did not say anything ; my father repeated it ; Clarkson did not answer.

My father said, save him, and then Clarkson raised up his hands to the blacks, and then they turned back. I heard a colored man, Ezekiel Thompson, say that he would as leave die as live. My father said he would kill him.

Mr. Brent asked what he meant by saying he.

Mr. Read objected to the question, on the ground that it was repeating the examination in chief, and that the witness could not tell whom his father meant.

Judge Grier said that it was evidently a grammatical error on the part of the boy. That he had used a pronoun of the third person singular, instead of the third person plural.

The witness, on being interrogated, said that he meant to have used the word *they* instead of *he*.

Judge Grier said that it was a very common error for witnesses to use the singular for the plural, when narrating a story to the court.

Witness : I saw Hanway going along the lane ; negroes were behind him shooting ; I did not see whom they were shooting at.

J. M. Read said that he would now fix the witnesses' position in the lane. For this purpose the counsel laid the plan before him, in order that he might point out the precise locality of the places named by him. This portion of the evidence was given to a select few, so that we were unable to obtain it. It was a matter more for Court than the Jury.

Witness : I stood in the first position about a quarter of an hour before I removed to the second.

J. Franklin Reigart, affirmed : I am an Alderman of the city of Lancaster ; I issued warrants for the arrest of Castner Hanway, Elijah Lewis and others.

J. M. Read here interposed and asked the counsel what he intended to prove by the witness.

Mr. Brent said that he wanted the witness to narrate a conversation which took place between the Marshal and Castner Hanway.

Witness : The warrant was in reality issued by Mr. Gihon, the affidavit was signed by me ; he got about fifty men and proceeded to the place ; they brought back Hanway and Lewis to Mr. Loker's ; while on the porch Mr. Kline went up to them and said : You white livered scoundrels, yesterday I pleaded to you like a dog for my life, and to stop the blacks from firing, and you would not ; Lewis answered that he had to fly for his life ; Hanway said nothing ; I went up and told him that he must not create any excitement there ; he answered that he could hardly suppress his feelings ; he, however, went away.

Cross-examined by Mr. Read : Has not Mr. Kline a formidable pair of whiskers.

Witness : I thought he was a very singular looking man.

Mr. Read asked other questions in regard to the personal appearance of Kline, which were stopped by the Court.

Cross-examined by J. M. Read : What did Kline say to you in regard to speaking to anybody to save his life. Mr. Read desired to show that he had before the Alderman said he had not heard either Hanway or Lewis speak a word on the ground of the fight, and that the occasion spoken of by the witness was a mere ebullition of passion on the part of Kline. Mr. Read asked that the affidavit be put in evidence.

Judge Grier said that he thought the matter was irrelevant. As Judge Kane was about to deliver his opinion, Mr. Read said that he would not press the matter upon the Court.

Witness: At the time I was taking the affidavit, before the warrant was issued, I saw Mr. Lewis on the spot, in the room; I saw Hanway on the ground with Lewis at the time the constable was dispatched in the crowd ; Lewis asked me if he might go to Lancaster ; I saw the constable serve the warrant about ten yards from the office, on both Hanway and Lewis.

Question by Mr. Brent: I think I saw Lewis in the room at the time Kline was giving his evidence in my office.

William Proudfoot sworn : I reside in Strasburg, Lancaster county ; I am a constable there ; the warrants for the arrest of Hanway, Lewis and others were placed in my hands ; I arrested Hanway and Lewis at Frederick Sicher's house in Christiana ; I was there a little before them ; I made the arrest myself ; Hanway and Lewis had come to Christiana ; I went out and took them into custody ; they asked me if they could not get off until to-morrow ; I told them I had no authority ; Kline came up to Hanway and said, You white-livered scoundrel, if you had said one word yesterday not one of our men would have been killed—you rather told them to shoot ! Hanway made no reply, but Elijah Lewis replied, I did not ; I heard nothing on either side about begging for lives.

Cross-examined by J. M. Read : I did not see Lewis and Hanway at Sicher's tavern before the warrants were issued ; I first saw them at the porch of Sicher's house ; it was known among the crowd that the deposition was taken for the purpose of making arrests. Lewis and Hanway were in the crowd.

Mr. Read asked the witness if he was personally willing that the prisoners should go to Lancaster until the next morning. Mr. Brent objected to the question.

Witness : They told me that they had been at the District

Attorney's, of Lancaster. They said that the District Attorney had nothing to do with it. I was not willing that they should go.

Charles Smith affirmed: I reside in Chester county, almost two miles from Christiana; I recollect the morning when Kline and the party came up; the morning when they came up a colored man—

Mr. Lewis stopped the witness at that point, and said that he supposed the witness was called to testify to the same as had been sworn to before Alderman Reigart, and that he had marked on the affidavit (which he handed to the Court), the parts to which he should object. I apprehend that this stands upon the same basis as any other conversation between third parties.

Judge Grier: It would not be irrelevant to show the fact that a person went from here to give notice to the neighborhood—but any conversation would perhaps be irrelevant.

Mr. Lewis: Such information might have been given by a stranger to the whole affair. There must be a connecting link, which there is not. This does not form part of the transaction; there has been no evidence and will be none to prove the connection of the defendant.

G. L. Ashmead: One of the witnesses stated that they met a colored man on going up, who followed Kline to Christiana. The same colored man, Samuel Williams, informed the witness on the stand that he had left a paper at Christiana containing the fact that persons were coming up to arrest slaves, and the names of those slaves. Mr. Ashmead said that they also intended to show that the blowing of horns at Parker's house and elsewhere was a preconcerted action to resist the authority of the United States.

J. W. Ashmead: He thought this one of the most important witnesses. They intended to prove that the said Samuel Williams had, instead of getting to Parker's house by mistake, went to another place, and there told the object of his visit to Christiana,

Mr. Lewis : If we look at the indictment it will be found that not a word is said of the man Williams, who has been mentioned.   It is to be recollected that Williams has not been connected in any way with the defendant.   We have a right to presume that the defendant was only on the ground as a spectator, which we will prove.   Your honor will perceive that it wants the connection between Williams and Hanway.   You must first show that the person charged is connected with the conspiracy, then you must give the conversation between the conspirators.   A man must not be implicated in the conspiracy by mere conversation between other parties than the one accused.   The defendant has not been connected with the affair as a conspirator.   They might with the same propriety have accused Mr. Knott, who arrived on the ground so soon, as to have implicated Castner Hanway.

Judge Kane : It is in evidence that the defendant was present at the time of the overt act.   The material question is the purpose for which he came—whether it was accidental or intentional.   Such evidence may be given as will enable the jury to infer the intention of the defendant in being there.

Judge Grier : We consider there is some prima facie evidence that this man was connected with the affair.   If a man is found armed, along with a hundred others, to resist the authority of the United States, you may possibly give in evidence that notices were given, speeches were made, and meetings were held.   The evidence was admitted.

Witness : The colored man came to my place about five o'clock in the morning ; his name was Samuel Williams ; he said that he had came up in the morning cars along with others who were after slaves, among who were Nelson and others, whose names he had on a piece of paper, at Christiana ; he said that he had come to my house in mistake for Boyd's.   He said he wished us to give the slaves notice that their masters were after them ; he said he left three names at Christiana ; Kline asked me to the assistance of Dickinson Gorsuch ; he said he would give $5 to anyone who would bring the bodies of Edward and his son ; I saw the body of Edward lying in the orchard ; I did not take him to my house ; I did not move him at all ; the inquest had not been held ; I left and went to Penningtonville.

Question by Mr. Brent : Did you see any of the wounds?

Witness : I saw only bleeding at the mouth ; he said he wished notice to be given to the slaves ; he used the word slaves ; I did not know where any of the slaves were ; I did not know ; he did not tell me from whom he got this information ; I did not ask him.

Cross-examined : Boyd's adjoins my place ; two miles from Parker's.

Dr. Augustus Cain affirmed : I reside near Christiana ; about 800 or 1,000 yards from that place ; it is about two and one-half miles from Parker's house ; on the 10th of September last, in the afternoon, Josephus Washington presented a paper to me with three names on it ; the first I do not recollect ; the second I do not know ; the second name was "Josh ;" the third name was Ford, with a dash after and under ; it was written Harford county, Maryland ; another colored man was with him.

Question by Mr. Brent : A colored man told me that the kidnapers were at Parker's ; it was six o'clock in the morning ; the first man that told me was Francis Harkins, a colored man ; I heard of the murder on the afternoon of that day ; I was called upon to dress the wounds of two colored persons on the forenoon of the day ; there were two—one was wounded in the arm, the other one in the thigh ; it was with balls ; I extracted them. I did not give the information ; one of them was named Henry C. Hopkins, the other John Longley ; it is likely I do know that a meeting was held where the Fugitive Slave law was taken into consideration ; it was held at West Chester, at the Horticultural Hall ; there were speeches made disapproving of the law.

Mr. Brent here presented the witness with a notice of a call for a meeting, published in one of the public newspapers. Mr. B. asked him if the resolutions published were the same as were passed.

Witness : I do not know ; I do not know who was chairman of the meeting ; I don't know whether Mr. Hanway was there ; I was not an officer of that meeting ; I think the meeting was held in the spring ; it was the Anti-Slavery Society which met there ; it was the annual convention ; I am not aware of any proceedings being published in any paper whatever ; I was there as a mere spectator.

Question by G. W. Ashmead : I dressed John Longley's wounds in a house of my tenant ; he was a light man, short and rather thin ; he did not tell me how he got hurt ; did not ask him ; Henry C. Hopkins occupied the house ; he is one of the men who was wounded ; the last time I saw them was the day of the murder ; they left the neighborhood immediately after ; my house was tenantless on that afternoon ; I did not know where John Longley resided.

John Roberts, a colored boy, sworn : I reside a mile the other side of Smyrna ; about three miles from Parker's house ; I have been in debtors' apartment seventy-two days ; there was a colored man in there with me named Josephus Washington, and another named John Clark ; they escaped from prison ; I don't know how they escaped ; I recollect the morning of the battle at Parker's house ; Joseph Scarlett came to my house about sun-up; he was on horseback ; he asked for my father ; my mother told him he was not at home ; he said that kidnapers were at Parker's, and to let the colored people know it ; I went to Joseph's house to tell them, but they were not at home ; I got a gun which I got from Joseph Townsend, a white man ; he loaded it for me ; I went to go to Parker's, and I got as far as George Irving's about eight o'clock ; I told Townsend that kidnapers were at Parker's.

No cross-examination.

Samuel Hanson, a colored boy, sworn: I live at William Regg's, about one and one-fourth miles from Christiana, and about two and a-half miles from Parker's; I was at the battle at Parker's awhile after sun-up; I got there after the fight was over; there were about fifty colored persons there; they were armed with guns, some of them; I heard a good deal of firing while coming down the lane; I saw Hanway between the little house and Parker's; no one lives in the small house; it is between Parker's and the creek; it is in the long lane; he was on horseback, going up the lane towards Pownall's house and the creek; I was about five or six yards from him; I was in the road coming up to the house; I passed Hanway; I did not speak to him; I had no arms with me; there were some negroes standing just alone, as if they were going away; there were some behind him; I went into the little lane apiece, when I started and came home; I saw the body of old Mr. Gorsuch; I was about one yard from him; I don't know whether he was dead; I went down to Christiana to get a pair of boots, when a man came along and said kidnapers were at Parker's; I met George Pownall coming up the road; he told me kidnapers were at Parker's; he is a white man; he was going away from Parker's house; when I first saw him he was coming towards Christiana; he did not go towards Parker's.

Cross-examination: I did not work for Isaac Moore. I was not at his house that day. After I was on the battle-ground I did not hear any firing. I am certain I saw Hanway; it was near the orchard that I saw him; I think he was riding down towards the creek.

Question by Mr. Brent: I want to understand this. You said you were going after a pair of boots?

Mr. Read interrupted the witness, in an objection to the question; he said that it would be nothing but a repetition of the evidence in chief, which would not be fair for the prisoner or justice.

Mr. Brent replied that the gentleman's idea of unfairness

suited only his view of the case ; if, after a cross examination, I am in doubt as to the precise points in the witness' evidence, I have a perfect right to be satisfied in all doubtful points.

Mr. Read said that he had great respect for the gentleman from Maryland, who had been sent here by that State to try these cases for the United States.

Mr. Read was here interrupted by Mr. Brent, who stated that the gentleman had made use of expressions which were irrelevant to the question. The gentleman said, I have been sent here by the State of Maryland, for the purpose of trying the cases of the United States ; I have been sent here by the Executive of Maryland as a representative of that State in the trial of cases which interest the entire community. I have been sent here, not because the trust reposed in Pennsylvania is thought unfit for that State ; no such thing. I am here to see that justice is done the memory of a citizen of one of the States of this Union.

Mr. Read made a few remarks in reply.

Judge Grier : You are both right in theory, but it would not answer for such a course to be made a rule ; for then there would be no end to an examination. A witness certainly has a right to explain himself. If there is anything obscure you may put your questions.

Witness : One white man passed me when I got at that little house ; I don't know who he was ; don't know whether I would know him again.

Jacob Woods sworn : I reside in Lancaster county at Jacob Moore's but I worked for Mr. Cooper; there were two farms lying between Moore's and Parker's house ; I mind the month in which the fight occurred ; but I don't mind the day ; I was at work at Mr. Cooper's on the morning of the battle, and I was going to take up potatoes ; Mr. Lewis came along and told me that kidnapers were over at Parker's ; it was after sun-up ; he told me it was no time to take up potatoes now, when William Parker's house was all surrounded by kidnapers ; I went over there with him ; the first I saw was the marshal and Mr. Hanway standing together near the mouth of the road ; I did not pass very close to them ; I did not hear anything pass between them ; I heard the noise of guns and saw the smoke ; when the firing took place, it kind of scared me, and I ran away towards the barn ; the marshal and Hanway were standing near the short lane ; I got into the corn fields and came out in the road by the woods ; I went straight over to Jacob Moore's where I get my washing done ; that is all I know about it. No cross examination.

Dickinson Gorsuch recalled. (A coat was here presented to the witness.) That is the coat which my father wore on that occasion, and that is the hat (which was also handed to him) worn by Dr. Pearce. The vest which the witness wore was also shown to the jury. The hole through the hat, which was made by a ball fired from Parker's window, was shown the jury. One of the preceding witnesses, it will be recollected, testified that the ball passed through Dr. Pearce's hat, injuring the scalp a little.

George L. Ashmead informed the Court that the testimony on the part of the United States had now closed.

John M. Read : As one of his colleagues was absent at Washington (Thaddeus Stevens), and as they had to rely upon the notes of the phonographers, which would not be ready until evening, he proposed that Mr. Cuyler should not commence the opening for the defense until morning.

Judge Grier replied that the only objection he had to the proposition was, that the jury empaneled might suppose that he was about to be liberal at the expense of their time. This was the only thing that caused him to hesitate, as by the employment of phonographers to take the testimony, they had already gained two days' time. It was so great an advantage that he had made up his mind never again to take notes himself of a case on trial.

The Court granted his request, and adjourned.

CHAPTER XIII.

TESTIMONY FOR THE DEFENSE.

THE TRIAL of Hanway was resumed Tuesday morning, December 2. Theodore C. Cuyler opened for the defense and commenced by reviewing the several Acts of the Assembly of Pennsylvania on this subject, and recapitulated the facts of the testimony which they would be able to present to the Court, upon which they confidently relied for an acquittal. Remarking upon the serious and unusual nature of the charge he said it had another point of deep interest, viz :

"The State of Maryland is here to-day, in the person of her Attorney General and his coadjutors—a private prosecutor in a criminal case. Far be it from me to say that she thirsts for the blood of this man ; and yet I have seen events occur upon the trial of this case which might almost justify this remark.

"It has ever been the merciful doctrine of the law, that the sworn officer of the law, its public prosecutor, was not justified in exhibiting the partisan zeal of private counsel, in pressing for a conjunction. This duty was to aid the Court in doing justice, to seek the disclosure of the whole truth, whether it makes for or against the Commonwealth, in short, to seek mercy, not sacrifice ; justice, not a conviction. How had it been in this case ?

"Mr. Ashmead, a proper officer of the Government, brings to every public and every professional duty, as we of the Philadelphia bar well know, at once the highest professional skill, and the most manly frankness and candor is in the background. Our friends from the State of Maryland, for whom no gentleman entertains a higher respect than I do, are in the foreground. Maryland distrusts the justice of Pennsylvania—she distrusts the faithfulness to their solemn duty of the officers of the General Government. She is here to-day in her own counsel in what she regards as her own case. As a natural result, we have witnessed precisely what experience taught us we might expect. This case, involving the momentous issues of life and death, has been tried as if it were a private case. In a panel of ninety-two attending jurors, the prisoner, entitled to thirty-four challenges, challenged twenty-four, while the Government (exercising a right by the most recent cases denied to a public prosecution in England) set aside thirty-six jurors.

"In the conduct of the case the zeal of private counsel has been exhibited—discharged witnesses have been recalled and cross-examined witnesses have been re-examined in chief, the opinions and impressions of witnesses have been asked for and put in proof as facts. And yesterday it was offered and received in proof to affect the prisoner, that by the lying lips of Henry H. Kline the prisoner and his fellow prisoner, Elijah Lewis, were charged in the vile profanity of that miserable creature, with what Kline knew and this prosecution admits was a lie, and his silence (Lewis denying the assertion) is to be ventured into a tacit admission of the truth of that which the prosecution itself admits is a false charge. Sir, I take back my words. The State of Maryland does thirst for blood, or else the case, inadmissible even in a Quarter Session practice, would not have been tried."

Mr. Cuyler stated that Castner Hanway was a native of the State of Delaware, but moved from there when five years old. He is no abolitionist and has no sympathies with them.

The speaker stated that they would prove that Mr. Hanway was upon the ground at Christiana for the purpose of putting down any disturbance which might arise. He would prove that Kline was in the woods, and did not see the occurrence

which he had detailed and sworn to. Mr. Hanway, it could
be proved, interposed his own body between Dr. Pearce and
danger, and it was to his exertions that the life of Dr. Pearce
was saved. The defendant further did all he could to stay the
acts of the rioters, and succeeded in restraining the blacks from
committing more extensive mischief.

He ridiculed the idea of such events as was detailed in the
evidence being held to be high treason, except when the law
was pronounced through the polluted lips of a Scroggs or a
Jeffries. He relied upon common-sense jurymen to throw
aside absurd theories.

After Mr. Cuyler closed, Elijah Lewis was affirmed, Mr.
Stevens stating that they intended to show by this witness that
anterior to the 11th of September there were overt acts committed by kidnapers in the vicinity of Christiana. Mr. Ashmead opposed the motion, on the ground of its irrelevancy—
the acts being some nine months before the riot.

After a long discussion, however, the evidence was admitted,
and Lewis detailed the circumstances of a party of white men
coming at night, in January, and by violence taking away a
black man from his son's house, after obtaining entrance by
stratagem. There was a panic and many negroes fled.

Henry Rhay testified to the same fact, showing that a pistol
was paraded, blood spilt, etc. Said he believed the negro was
from Maryland, and named John, but the men made no statement about his being a runaway slave. Adjourned.

The trial of Castner Hanway was resumed Wednesday,
December 3, in the United States Circuit Court—Judges Grier
and Kane.

Thompson Loughead sworn : I live in Strasburg township ;
on the morning of this affair at Parker's I heard of the
rumpus ; I came around the road by the woods ; within fifteen
or twenty yards of the road I heard guns, one after another ; I
passed over into the road, about one hundred and fifty yards ;
there I met Elijah Lewis ; he said to me, you had better go

back; a man came down from the woods and hallooed out, hold on! stop! I turned around to go back; I went over the cornfield; Lewis went by the road; I met Joseph Scarlett by the mill; the marshal came up and asked the way to Penningtonville; he said that two men were wounded, one of whom was in the woods; he asked something about a doctor; he said he thought one of them was fatally wounded. I said, Why did you stay so long when the blacks were gathering? He said, That's what I told them, but they would not come off; he said that he was tired; that he came from Philadelphia the night before; I looked down to his hands, and saw they were drabbled.

Isaac Rodgers affirmed: On the morning, (I live about 800 yards from Parker's up the long lane,) I heard a noise over at Parker's house, about sunrise on Thursday morning; I ran down as far as the creek; I stood there a few minutes, and heard a great firing of guns; I started to go back, when I saw Castner riding down alongside of Dr. Pearce; a colored man was following them with a gun; I cried out not to shoot; Hanway turned around several times and said, Don't shoot, boys; they were between the creek and my house.

Joseph C. Dickeson affirmed: On the day after the murder of Mr. Gorsuch I and Dr. Pearce took the cars for Lancaster; he sat on the same seat beside me; he said that it was the rashest piece of business he ever knew; the old man had behaved imprudently, and that Kline did not act right; he said that he called several times for Kline; that the old man came out of the lane with a changed countenance; he was calm and resolute. The old gentleman said he would have his slaves or die in the attempt; that he, the old man, wheeled round, and fell from a wound; that Dickinson Gorsuch fell at the same time. He also said that he came up to Hanway, who turned to the blacks and said, For God's sake, don't shoot, and that he believed that Hanway saved his life. He said Kline left before the firing; he blamed Kline very much.

Cross-examined by Mr. Brent: He blamed the old man Gorsuch for both his own death and that of his son's. He said that he persuaded the old man to leave ; that he was rash. I don't recollect of his saying that the blacks were too numerous for them ; he showed me his wound ; he said that he kept alongside of Mr. Hanway ; he did not state his object in doing so. I don't know whether he said the negroes obeyed him.

Dr. Patterson affirmed : On the evening of the same day of the riot I saw Dr. Pearce at the house of Levi Pownall, where he was attending his cousin, who was wounded. He said that while he was retreating he met Hanway, whom he believed saved his life from the infuriated blacks who were pursuing him. His language to me was conclusive. He spoke to me of Hanway saving his life. He said that he believed he owed his life to Hanway, and that, before he got to the ground, Kline told him of his former feats of valor, which led him to believe he was exceedingly great ; but when the danger presented itself his courage forsook him.

James G. Henderson affirmed : I heard Dr. Pearce relate to others concerning Kline at the fight, on the morning of the fight. He said that the marshal had acted cowardly ; that he had left the ground, which encouraged the blacks to fire.

The witnesses for the defense, who were examined in the case of Hanway, gave testimony principally as to the bad character and general untruthfulness and want of veracity of Henry H. Kline, the principal witness for the prosecution, who was the special deputy marshal for arresting the negroes. The following persons were successively examined :

Judge W. D. Kelly, Francis Jobson, W. D. Franks, David Evans, George Simpson, Isaac G. Stratton, William Shorods, Jacob Walker, John Hinkle, Norman Ackley, Anthony Hoover, Aaron B. Fithian, George K. Wise, John Miche, Andrew Redhiffer, Jacob Albright, Lewis Cooper, John Carr, John S. Cochran, William McClimans, Thomas Lister, James

Smith, William S. Nutt, John Muderson, Jacob Glasmire, John Houston, John W. Dittus and Joseph L. Parker. Among the rest Judge Kelly said:

I am acquainted with Henry H. Kline, of this city. I believe I know his general character for truth and veracity. It is very bad. It would depend on circumstances whether I would believe him on his oath.

Most of the Philadelphia witnesses had quite as bad an opinion of Kline as Judge Kelly had, and many worse, and would not believe him on oath. Some of these witnesses, who lived at Christiana, also testified to its being usual to blow horns in that neighborhood, of a morning, to waken the laborers.

Three of the above witnesses—Carr, Cochran and McClimans—were called to show that the sworn statement of Kline, that he saw Harvey Scott, negro, at Christiana in the riot, was totally false, and that he was four miles from the spot. They affirmed that G. W. Harvey Scott slept at Carr's house the night previous, and was there the next morning.

Lewis Cooper affirmed: I did go to Parker's the morning of the affray. When I got there I saw Joseph Scarlett with Dickinson Gorsuch by the roadside. Mr. Gorsuch was wounded. Scarlett was giving him drink, holding his head and keeping the sun off. I asked where the men were who were wounded. He pointed to Mr. Gorsuch, and said his father was dead. I proposed to take him in my dearborn. Scarlett and I put him in, and sat on each side of him. We took him to Pownall's, where he was made as comfortable as possible. I asked Mr. Gorsuch if there were any white men assisting the negroes. He said there were none.

Enoch Haslan testified to the general character of Castner Hanway as a good, peaceable and loyal citizen, whom he had known for twenty-eight years.

On Thursday, December 4, the defense produced some dozen witnesses to prove the character of Hanway as a peaceful and

ELIJAH LEWIS.

orderly citizen, and of very good character. The defense here closed their testimony.

George L. Ashmead said that it now became his duty to open the rebutting evidence of the United States.

The rebutting testimony of the United States then commenced. Innumerable witnesses were introduced, one after the other, who emphatically swore to the general good character of Kline, and that they relied upon his truth and veracity, and would believe him upon oath as readily as any other man. Most of them had known Kline from eight to twenty-five years. Some of the witnesses were aldermen, others officers, and of various callings.

By agreement the further examination of witnesses as to Kline's character was here suspended.

The United States offered to show the state of feeling in Christiana long previous to the present disturbance, and that armed bands of whites and blacks had paraded the country to oppose the law of Congress.

A long discussion arose on this point, and it was finally over-ruled by the Court. Another witness was called to show that the negro alleged to have been abducted was a runaway slave, and this was overruled. Harvey Scott, negro, was called on to state what took place at or about Parker's house during the fight ; and although he had previously made two affidavits in regard to the circumstances, yet, when he came to testify positively, he denied having been there, and said he had made the statement through fear. This ended all testimony.

The plea of Mr. Read in behalf of the prisoner was of great length and of profound ability. On the law of treason he was remarkably cogent and convincing. Mr. Stevens, whom multitudes were most anxious to hear, deemed it best—so well had the defense been sustained by his colleague, and so weak was the cause of the prosecution—to forbear speaking. His decision, much as it disappointed his numerous friends, was dictated by a wise regard of the circumstances by which he was surrounded, and especially for the patience of the jury, already too severely taxed.

Mr. Ludlow then summed up for the United States—stated that the United States did not seek innocent blood—declared the charge was founded in the Constitution, sustained by the law, and proved by the facts of the case. He reviewed the evidence already adduced, and concluded by denouncing those fanatics and demagogues who had excited this treasonable outbreak, and who had been employed for years in attempts to overthrow the Government, and strike from the firmament of nations the sun which had illumiuated them all. The prisoner, said he, answered when asked how he would be tried, "By God and my country." You, gentlemen of the jury, represent that country, but in your deliberations be guided by that Deity who presides over the destinies of our nation. If the prisoner is innocent, let him be acquitted—if guilty, let him fall.

Mr. Lewis summed up for the defense. He stated the position of Pennsylvania in regard to slavery, and asked if a free black citizen of Pennsylvania was found in a Southern State, he was not liable to imprisonment? He said :

"Pennsylvania puts no obstruction in the way of reclaiming fugitives, but only her own free citizens should not be unlawfully carried off. Was not this the position of Castner Hanway? Did he not act only as a Pennsylvanian should act? The whole evidence showed that he had only endeavored to see that no kidnaping was going on.

"Our law merely says that no man can be carried into slavery, if a free man ; and, if a slave, that no obstruction should be placed in their way. This was the position of the prisoner. Is there a single thing he did but in accordance with his Pennsylvania feeling and Pennsylvania rights? There is no man that regrets this catastrophe more than Castner Hanway ; that a citizen of Maryland should have been shot down, is regretted by him as by all others. This is shown by his direction to his counsel, that no question should be asked of the two members of the Gorsuch family, who appeared to give evidence in this case.

"The charge of treason—the continent from ocean to ocean is 3000 miles broad, and from the St. Lawrence to the Rio Grande, not less than 2000—and the extent of territory in this country is but a few acres wide ; the occurrence was in the township of Sadsbury, between a corn-field and an orchard. Was not this an excellent place to raise an army? And this occurrence in the township of Sadsbury is treason ! This was to overturn the General Government ! Why, the accusation is so ridiculously absurd, that all that is needed is to hold the matter up to view.

"We are not trying the Fugitive Slave law. The Fugitive Slave law is trying itself. We apprehend that the South will be the first to be dissatisfied. That every man carried back to slavery will be an apostle of liberty, and the South will ask as a boon that which she would now resist." He alluded to the opening remarks of the counsel of the United States relative to the stability of the Union.

It was founded on the affections of the people ; and he held that the continually talking about the instability and destruction of the Union looked much more like treason than anything which Castner Hanway had done.

Mr. Brent opened for the United States, contending that the Compromise law imposed an active duty on the North in returning fugitive slaves. The man refusing to assist is a disloyal citizen. The prisoner did not confine himself to this, however, but became a conspirator, inciting the colored men to resistance and bloodshed by words and gestures.

Mr. Cooper closed the case for the government, or rather the state of Maryland, which had no fair title to be heard at all. He doubtless earned his fee, but he added nothing to his reputation which a good man might covet, and less than nothing to help the hopeless cause of his client.

CHAPTER XIV.

JUDGE GRIER'S CHARGE TO THE JURY.

THE CHARGE of Judge Grier has always been regarded as a remarkable specimen of judicial literature, and it is here given in full. Considering the circumstances under which it was pronounced, and the high position of the author, it is worthy of careful examination. Such language as he employed in describing the scene at Christiana was as unworthy of the Bench, as it was untrue in fact. The application to such persons as Lucretia Mott, Abby Kelley Foster, Mary Grew, William Lloyd Garrison and Charles and Cyrus Burleigh, of such terms as "male and female vagrant lecturers," and "infuriated fanatics and unprincipled demagogues," would have excited no surprise if the speaker had been a bar-room politician, and his audience a company of rowdies ; but what shall be said of such language, applied to such persons, by a Judge of the Supreme Court of the United States? Must not every right-minded citizen have hung his head for shame in view of such aspersions from a Court of high jurisdiction? But the reader will be abundantly able to make his own comments upon a document so deficient in moral principle and judicial dignity, and which abounds in flippant and gratuitous calumny upon individuals who were not upon trial, and of whose principles and plans the author knew nothing, save what he had gathered from the misrepresentations of their enemies. His remarks follow :

GENTLEMEN OF THE JURY :—We must commend the patient attention which you have thus far given to this most important and interesting case. It has taken up much of your time and caused you some personal inconvenience, but not more perhaps than the importance of the issue, both as respects the interests of the public and your duty to the prisoner whom you have in charge has necessarily required.

It has been the anxious desire of the Court, notwithstanding the pressure of other duties, to give ample time and opportunity for the careful and full investigation of the facts and law, bearing on the case—not only because it is the first of a numerous list of cases of the same description which involve the issue of life and death to the parties immediately concerned, but because we know that the public eye is fixed upon us and demands at our hands the unprejudiced and impartial performance of the solemn duties which we have been called to execute.

The prisoners at the bar have a right to require of you that you should not permit the atrocity of the transaction or your horror of the offense with which he is charged, or your proper desire to vindicate the insulted laws of the country, to cause you to forget your duties to him, and convict him without full and satisfactory proof of his guilt.

The Government also, while it cannot desire the sacrifice of an innocent individual for the purpose of public example, has a right to demand of you a firm, a fearless, and unflinching performance of your duty, and that the verdict you shall render shall be a true verdict, according to the evidence which you have heard, and the law as explained to you by the Court.

Before proceeding to notice more particularly the questions of law or fact arising in this case, or the defendant's complicity in the transaction, suffer me to advert to some matters, which, though only historically known to us, yet having passed before our eyes, as citizens of the Commonwealth, may have a tendency to create in our minds some bias on this subject, but which should not be permitted to affect your verdict, whatever your private sentiments and feelings may happen to be.

Without intimating any opinion as to the guilt or innocence of the prisoner at the bar, it must be admitted that the testimony in this case has clearly established that a most horrible outrage upon the laws of the country has been committed.

A citizen of a neighboring state, while in the exercise of his undoubted rights guaranteed to him by the Constitution and laws of the United States, has been foully murdered by an armed mob of negroes. Others have been shot down, beaten, wounded, and have, with difficulty, escaped with their lives. An officer of the law, in the execution of his duty, has been openly repelled by force and arms.

All this has been done in open day—in the face of a portion of the citizens of this Commonwealth, whose bounden duty it was as good citizens to support the execution of the laws without any opposition on their part—without any attempt at interference to preserve the peace; and who, if they did not directly encourage or participate in the outrage, looked carelessly and coldly on. These, I say, are facts established in the case beyond contradiction.

That it is the duty, either of the State of Pennsylvania or of the United States, or of both, to bring to condign punishment those who have committed this flagrant outrage on the peace and dignity of both, cannot be doubted.

It is now more than sixty years since the adoption of the Constitution of the United States. Under its benign influence we have become a great and powerful nation ; happy and prosperous at home ; feared and respected abroad. And why has this confederacy obtained such an immeasurable superiority over the other republics on this continent ? It is because, here, all bow to the supremacy of the law—because, here, we have a moral, virtuous, and a religious people, and a firm, fearless and impartial administration of the law—because, here, the minority uphold the constitutions and laws imposed by the majority—because we have not here pronunciamentos, rebellions and civil wars, caused by the lust of power, by the ignorance of faction or fanaticism, which in other countries have marred every attempt at free government.

That the people of the great state of Pennsylvania have a loyality, fidelity, and love to this Union and the Constitution and laws which have so exalted us as a nation cannot be doubted ; and yet I grieve to admit, that the only trials and convictions on record for armed and treasonable resistance to the laws of the United States since the adoption of the constitution have their venue laid in Pennsylvania.

But these were more than fifty years ago, and before we had become accustomed to the working of a new and untried experiment in self government, or anticipated its glorious results. It is not our purpose to excuse or vindicate those early outbreaks of popular insubordination which were soon suppressed by military force and the impartial execution of the laws by courts and juries.

But without, at present, expressing any opinion whether the present outrage is to be classed under the legal catgeory of riot, murder or treason, we think it due to the reputation of the people of this commonwealth, to say that (with the exception of a few individuals of perverted intelligence, some small districts or neighborhoods whose moral atmosphere has been tainted and poisoned by male and female vagrant lecturers and conventions,) no party in politics, no sect of religion of any respectable numbers or character can be found within our borders who have viewed with approbation or looked with any other than feelings of abhorrence upon this disgraceful tragedy.

It is not in this Hall of Independence, that meetings of infuriated fanatics and unprincipled demagogues have been held to counsel a bloody resistance to the laws of the land. It is not in this city that conventions are held denouncing the constitution, the laws, and the Bible. It is not here that the pulpit has been desecrated by seditious exhortations, teaching that theft is meritorious, murder excusable and treason a virtue.

The guilt of this foul murder rests not alone on the deluded individuals who were its immediate perpetrators, but the blood taints with even deeper dye the skirts of those who promulgate doctrines subversive of all morality and all government.

This murderous tragedy is but the necessary development of principles and the natural fruit from seed sown by others whom the arm of the law cannot reach.

In making these remarks, we prefer to speak the truth in plain language, without seeking for bland euphemisms or flattering terms of respect for the promulgators of principles which we verily believe are not only dangerous to the peace, prosperity and happiness of the citizens of these United States, and tending to the dissolution of the Union, but subversive of all human government.

I have adverted to these matters which must have forced themselves on our minds and attention before the commencement of this trial, in order to warn you also against suffering them to bias your minds in this case. The defendant must stand or fall, by the evidence in the case, and not be made the scape-goat or sacrifice for the offenses of others unless he be proved to have participated in them. But if that shall have been made to appear by the evidence, it will be no excuse or defense for him, that others are equally guilty with himself. It is due to him, however, to say that their is no evidence before us that the prisoner attended any of these conventions got up to fulminate curses against the Constitution and laws of the country, to libel its best citizens and to exhort to a seditious and bloody resistance to the execution of its laws.

You will have observed that this bill of indictment charges the defendant with treason in resisting the execution of a certain law of Congress concerning fugitives from labor, which has been the subject of much controversy and agitation, and on which it may be proper to make a few remarks before we proceed to the more immediate merits of the case.

The learned counsel for the prisoner, having a due regard for the high character which they sustain in their profession, have not made the objection to this law which has been so clamorously urged by many presses and agitators, that it is unconstitutional. It is true that some ecclesiastical assemblies in the north, treating it, we presume, as a question of theology or orthodoxy have ventured to anticipate the decision of the legal tribunals on this subject. But highly as we respect their opinions on all questions properly within their cognizance, we cannot receive their decisions as binding precedents on questions arising under the Constitution.

The Constitution enacts that "no person held to service or labor in one State under the laws thereof escaping into another, shall, in consequence of any law or regulation therein, be discharged from such service or labor, but shall be delivered up on claim of the party to whom such service or labor may be due." This is the supreme law of the land, binding not only the respective States as such, but on the conscience and conduct of every individual citizen of the United States. It is well known that without this clause, the assent of the Southern States could never have been obtained to this compact of Union. And it, contrary to good faith, it should be practically nullified—if individuals or State legislatures in the North can succeed in thwarting and obstructing the execution of this article of our confederation and the rights guaranteed to the South thereby, they have no right to complain if the people in the South should treat the Constitution as virtually annulled by the consent of the North, and seek secession from any alliance with open and avowed covenant breakers.

Every compact must have mutuality ; it must bind in all its parts and all its parties or it binds none. Those States in the North whose legislation has made it a penal offense for their judicial and executive officers to lend their assistance in the execution of this clause of the Constitution, and compels them to disregard their solemn oath to support it, have proceeded as far, and perhaps further, in the path of nullification and secession than any Southern State has yet done. I know it is attempted to justify such legislation by casting the blame on the Supreme Court of the United States, and quoting certain dicta of some of the judges in the case of the Commonwealth vs. Prigg.

The question before the Court in that case, and the only question which could be decided was this and this only: "That the master of a fugitive having a right under the Constitution, to arrest his slave without writ, and take him away, any State legislation which interfered with, or obstructed that right, and (as in the case before the Court) punished the master or his agent as a kidnaper, was void." How such a decision can justify such legislation it is not easy to perceive.

The Act of Congress of 1793, which was first made to enforce this clause of the Constitution, was found to be defective and inoperative; and chiefly because it provided no legal process or public officer to make the arrest of the fugitive and bring him before the magistrate.

The forcible arrest and seizure of a man without any writ or semblance of legal authority, justly became odious, because it was liable to very great abuse. There was nothing to distinguish the arrest of a master from the seizure of the vile kidnaper and man-stealer. The Act of 1850 remedies this evil; it gives the master legal process and an officer of the law to make the arrest, and moreover gives the party arrested the benefit of a hearing and the decision of a judicial officer, before he can be deported. The free colored man who was before liable to capture by kidnapers, is better protected by this law than he was before.

In this feature alone is there any characteristic difference between this Act and the Act of 1793, to which it is a supplement? No objection had ever been urged to that Act, that it was unconstitutional, because it did not give the alleged fugitive a jury trial. In no cases of extradition, either of fugitives from justice or from labor, where the only question to be decided is the identity of the person whose reclamation is sought, had it ever been heard that the country or state to which he fled, was to try the question of his guilt or innocence, or pass upon his rights and duties in the state from which he fled. And yet this newly discovered argument is the only one which has ever been urged, with any pretense even to plausibility, by those who make so great clamor against this Act.

The truth is, the shout of disapprobation with which this Act has been received by some has been caused, not because it is injurious or dangerous to the rights of freemen of color in the Northern States, or is unconstitutional; but because it is an Act which can be executed and the constitutional rights of the master in some measure preserved. The real objection with these persons is the Constitution itself, which is supposed to be void of this particular from the effect of some "higher law" whose potential influence can equally annul all human and divine law.

It is true that the number of persons whose consciences affect to be governed by such a law is very small. But there is a much larger number who take up opinions on trust or by contagion, and have concluded this must be a very pernicious and unjust enactment, for no other reason, than because the others shout their disapprobation with such violence and vituperation. And possibly some might be found who affect to join the chorus with some slight hopes that they may be able to ride into place and power on the waves created by continual agitation.

It may not be said of this law, or perhaps of any other, that it is perfect, or the best that could possibly be enacted, or that it is incapable of amendment. But this may truly be said that while there are so many discordant opinions on the subject, it is not probable that a better compromise will be made; and probably none of us will live to see any act on this subject made to please every one.

Let it suffice for the present to say to you, gentlemen of the jury, that this law is constitutional; that the question of its constitutionality is to be settled by the courts and not by conventions either of laymen or ecclesiastics; that we are as much bound to support this law as any other, and that public armed opposition to the execution of this law is as much treason as it would be against any other act of Congress to be found in our statute books.

Let us now proceed to examine more particularly the specific charges laid in this bill of indictment, the evidence given to support them, and the question of law involved in the case.

The bill of indictment charges that the prisoner, Castner Hanway, wickedly intending and devising the peace and tranquility of the United States to disturb and prevent the execution of the laws thereof, to wit : "An act respecting fugitives from justice and persons escaping from the service of their masters," approved February 12, 1793, and another act supplementary to the same, passed on the 18th of September, 1850, did on the 11th of September, 1851, wickedly and traitorously intend to levy war against the United States.

It then sets forth five several overt acts.

1. That with a large number of persons armed and arrayed with warlike weapons, with purpose to oppose and prevent by means of intimidation and violence the execution of said laws, he did wickedly and traitorously levy war against United States.

2. That in pursuance of said purpose the prisoner and others so armed and traitorously assembled to prevent the execution of said laws, did with force and arms traitorously resist one Henry H. Kline, an officer of the United States, duly appointed, from executing lawful process, and wickedly and traitorously did prevent by force and intimidation, the execution of the said laws.

3. The third is the same with the second, with this addition, that they assaulted Kline and liberated from his custody persons arrested by him, who owed service and labor to Edward Gorsuch under the laws of Maryland, thereby traitorously preventing the execution of said laws.

4. That the prisoner with the others did traitorously meet, conspire, and consult to oppose, resist and prevent by force the execution of said law.

5. That in pursuance of said traitorous intention he prepared

divers books, letters, resolutions addresses, etc., which he caused to be dispersed, containing incitements and encouragements to fugitives and others to resist, oppose and prevent by violence and intimidation the execution of said laws.

Whether the allegations of this bill of indictment are supported by evidence, is the matter which you are sworn to try.

In assisting you to arrive at a correct conclusion on these points, it is not the intention of the Court to intimate an opinion on any disputed fact. These are to be decided by the jury on their own responsibility and the oath they have respectively taken to give a true verdict.

But there are certain facts in the case which have not been disputed by the learned counsel, and which, in speaking of this case, we may assume to have been satisfactorily proved, as they have not been denied. They are these :

That Edward Gorsuch, a citizen of Maryland, was the owner of certain slaves, or persons held to labor by the laws of that State. That these slaves had escaped and fled into Pennsylvania, and were known to be lurking in the neighborhood of the village of Christiana, in Sadsbury township, Lancaster county. That Edward Gorsuch came to Philadelphia in September last, and obtained warrants for the arrest of these fugitives from E. D. Ingraham, Esq., a Commissioner of this Court, having authority by law to issue such warrants. That these warrants were put into the hands of Henry H. Kline, an officer duly authorized to execute them.

That on the morning of the 11th of September, about daylight, the officer, Henry H. Kline, accompanied by Edward Gorsuch, his son Dickinson Gorsuch, his nephew Dr. T. Pearce, his cousin J. M. Gorsuch, and Nicholas Hutchins and Nathan Nelson, citizens of Maryland, proceeded to the house of one Parker.

That a person who was recognized as one of the fugitives for whom the warrants had been issued, was seen to come out of the house.

That the fugitive, on seeing the officer and his company, immediately fled into the house and upstairs, leaving the door open behind him. That Mr. Gorsuch pursued him, followed by the officer.

That a number of negroes were collected upstairs, armed in various ways, and determined to resist the capture of the fugitives. That a gun was fired by one of them at Mr. Gorsuch, and others of his assailants were struck with missiles thrown from the upper windows. That a pistol was then fired by the officer, not aimed at the negroes, but rather to frighten them and let them know their assailants were armed.

That a parley was then held between the parties, and the negroes informed that the officer had legal process in his hands for their arrest. That the negroes demanded time for the purpose, as was supposed, of offering terms of surrender, but in reality, perhaps, to gain time for the arrival of assistance from the neighborhood. That after some lapse of time the defendant arrived on the ground, and at the same time or soon after, large numbers of negroes began to collect around with various weapons of offense, such as guns, clubs, scythes and corn cutters.

That on the arrival of these reinforcements the persons in the house set up a yell of defiance. That the officer made known his character, and exhibited his writs to the defendant and another white man, who had arrived on the ground, and demanded their assistance in executing the warrants, which was refused. That the officer, deeming the attempt to execute his writs in the face of a numerous, armed, and angry mob of negroes, made no further attempt to do so, being content to escape with his life.   •

That the mob of armed negroes, now amounting to near or about one hundred persons, immediately made an attack upon the party who attended the officer. Edward Gorsuch was then shot down, beaten with clubs, and murdered on the spot. His son, who came to his assistance, was shot and wounded, and with difficulty escaped with his life.

Dr. Pearce, the nephew, was surrounded and beaten, but escaped with his life.

It is in evidence, also, and not disputed, that on the preceding evening notice had been given in the neighborhood by a negro who had followed the officer from Philadelphia, that an arrest of the fugitives was intended, and that the concourse and riot of the morning was evidently by preconcert and in consequence of such information.

Without at present noticing the further history of the transaction or expressing any opinion of the conduct of the white people in the neighborhood on the occasion, or of the miserable farce of the jury of inquest, got up as an afterpiece to this disgraceful tragedy, we may say that the evidence has clearly shown that the participants in this transaction are guilty of riot and murder at least—whether the crime amounts to treason or not will be presently considered.

Two questions present themselves for your inquiry:

Was the defendant, Castner Hanway, a participant in the offenses proved to have been committed? Did he aid, abet, or assist the negroes in this transaction, without regard to the grade or description of the offense committed?

And secondly, if he did, was the offense treason against the United States, as alleged in this bill of indictment?

The first one of these questions is one wholly of fact and for your decision alone. The last is a mixed question of law and fact. On the law you have a right to look to the Court for a correct definition of what constitutes treason, but whether the defendant has committed an offense which comes within that category, is, of course, a matter of fact for your decision.

When a murder is committed all who are present aiding, abetting and assailing, are equally guilty with him who gave the fatal stroke.

An abettor of a murder in order to be held liable as a principal in the felony, must be present at the transaction; if he be absent he may be an accessory. But in treason all are principals, and a man may be guilty of aiding and abetting though not present.

" If one man watch while another breaks into a house at night and robs it, both are guilty of burglary."

" If A comes and kills a man and B runs with an intent to assist him, if there should be occasion, though in fact he doth nothing, yet he is a principal, being present as well as A."

" If divers persons come with one assent to do mischief, as to kill, rob or beat, and one doeth it, they are all principals in the felony."

" If many be present and one only gives the stroke, whereof the party dies, they are all principals."

" Thus if two fight a duel, and one of them is killed, the seconds who are present are both guilty of murder."

" If A and B be fighting, and C, a man of full age, comes, by chance, and is a looker-on only, and assists neither, he is not guilty of murder or manslaughter, but it is a mis-prision for which he shall be fined, unless he uses means to apprehend the felon."

Lastly, " If divers persons come in one company, to do any unlawful thing, as to kill, rob, or beat a man, or commit a riot, or to do any other trespass, and one of them in doing thereof kill a man, this shall be adjudged murder in them all that are present of that party abetting him and consenting to the act, or ready to aid him, although they did but look on."

I have given you these examples from the books, in order that you may form some idea as to the nature of what the law treats as criminal aiding, abetting and countenancing the perpetration of an offense.

In the present case, the defendant, Castner Hanway, was present, as proved by several witnesses and not denied. But did he come to aid, abet, countenance, or encourage the rioters? If so, he was guilty of every act committed by any individual engaged in the riot—whether it amounts to felony or treason.

There is no evidence of any previous connection of the prisoner with this party before the time the offense was committed—that he had counselled, advised, or exhorted the negroes to come together with arms and resist the officer of the law or murder his assistants.

There is no evidence even that the prisoner was a member of any of these associations or conventions, which occasionally or annually infest the neighboring village of West Chester, for the purpose of railing at and reviling the Constitution and laws of the land, and denouncing those who execute them as no better than a Scroggs and a Jeffries—who stimulate and exhort poor negroes to the perpetration of offenses which they know must bring them to the penitentiary or the gallows.

The fact of his interference, whether active or passive, of his aiding, counselling, or abetting the perpetrators of this offense, has been argued from this language and conduct during its perpetration in his presence.

His acts, his declarations and his conduct are fair subjects for your careful examination, in order to judge of his intentions or his guilty complicity with those whose hands perpetrated the offense. If, as the counsel for the United States have argued, he countenanced or encouraged, aided or abbetted the offenders in the commission of the offense, he is equally guilty with them.

If, on the contrary, as is argued by his counsel, he came there without any knowledge of what was about to take place, and took no part by encouraging, countenancing, or aiding the perpetrators of the offense—if he merely stood neutral through fear of bodily harm, or because he was conscientiously scrupulous about assisting to arrest a fugitive from labor, and therefore merely refused to interfere while he did not aid or encourage the offenders, he may not have acted the part of a good citizen, he may be liable to punishment for such neutrality by fine and imprisonment, but he cannot be said to be liable as a principal in the riot, murder and treason committed by the others—and much more so if, as has been argued, his only interference was to preserve the lives of the officer and his attendants.

A man may have such conscientious principles on the subject of non-resistance as to stand by with indifference and neutrality when his father or friend is attacked by a bear or a madman, and in case of his death may not be liable as an aider or abettor in the murder or manslaughter. We may wonder at his philosophic indifference, though we cannot admire the man.

So a man who is a mere spectator in a contest where a mob of rioters are resisting an officer of the law in the execution of his duty, may refuse assistance, countenance or aid to either side. In so doing he is not acting the part of an honest, loyal citizen ; he may be liable to be punished for a misdemeanor for his refusal to interfere, but such conduct will not necessarily make him liable as a principal in the riot or murder committed. But such conduct is a fair subject for the consideration of a jury in connection with other circumstances to show preconcert and guilty complicity with the rioters, murderers or traitors.

What inference the jury may draw from the evidence in this case, of the conduct of this prisoner, is for them to say, after carefully weighing the arguments which have been so ably argued by the learned counsel.

With these remarks we submit this point of the case to the jury, after reading to them, if they desire it, the testimony of the witnesses bearing more directly on this question.

If you should find that the defendant, Castner Hanway, did not aid, assist or abet in the perpetration of the offense, you will return a verdict of not guilty, without regard to the grade or the offense, whether riot, murder or treason. But if you should find that he has so aided and abetted so as thereby to become a principal in the transaction according to the rules of law which we have first stated, you will next have to inquire whether the offense, as proved, amounts to the crime of "Treason against the United States."

The bill charges the defendant with "wickedly and traitorously intending to levy war against the United States," and the jury must find the act or acts to have been committed with such intention. For although the prisoner may have been guilty of riot, robbery, murder or any other felony, he cannot be found guilty under this bill of indictment, unless you find that he intended to levy war against the United States, or that the acts were committed by himself and others in pursuance of some conspiracy or preconcert for that purpose; and this is a question of fact for the decision of the jury. But in the decision of it the jury should regard the construction of the Constitution as given them by the Court as to what is the true meaning of the words "levying war."

Treason against the United States is defined by the Constitution itself. Congress has no power to enlarge, restrain, construe or define the offense. Its construction is entrusted to the Court alone.

By this instrument it is declared that "Treason against the United States shall consist only in levying war against them, or in adhering to their enemies, giving them aid and comfort. No person shall be convicted of treason unless on the testimony of two witnesses to the same overt act, or on confession in open Court."

What constitutes "levying war against the Government," is a question which has been the subject of much discussion whenever an indictment has been tried under this article of the Constitution.

The offense is described in very few words, and in their application to particular cases much difference of opinion may be expected.

We derive our laws as well as our language from England. As we would apply to English dictionaries and classical writers to ascertain the proper meaning of a particular word, so when we would inquire after the true definition of certain legal phraseology we would naturally look to the text writers and judicial decisions which we know that the framers of our Constitution would regard as the standard authorities in questions of legal definition. Otherwise the language of the Constitution on this subject might be subject to any construction which the passion or caprice of a Court and jury might choose to give it in times of public excitement.

At one time the Constitution might be nullified by a narrow construction, and at another time the life and liberty of the citizen be sacrificed by a latitudinous one.

"The term levying war," says Chief Justice Marshall, "is not for the first time applied to treason by the Constitution of the United States. It is a technical term. It is used in a very old statute of that country whose language is our language, and whose laws form the sub-stratum of our laws. It is scarcely conceivable that the term was not employed by the framers of our Constitution in the sense which has been affixed to it by those from whom we borrowed it. So far as the meaning of any terms, particularly terms of art, is completely ascertained, those by whom they are employed must be considered as employing them in their ascertained meaning, unless the contrary is proved by the context."

Since the adoption of the Constitution but few cases of indictment for treason have occurred and most of those not many years afterwards. Many of the English cases then considered good law, and quoted by the best text writers as authorities, have since been discredited if not overruled in that country. The better opinion there at present seems to be that the term "levying war" should be confined to insurrections and rebellions for the purpose of overturning the Government by force and arms. Many of the cases of constructive treason, quoted by Foster, Hale, and other writers, would, perhaps, now be treated merely as aggravated riots or felonies. But for the purpose of the present case it is not necessary to pursue this subject further or to look beyond the case decided in our country. This subject is one of too serious importance to allow this Court to indulge in speculations of our own or wander from the safe path of precedent.

In England all insurrections to imprison the King, or to force him to change his measures, or to remove counsellors ; to attack his troops in opposition to his authority ; to carry off or destroy his stores provided for defense of his realm ; if done conjointly with or in aid of rebels and not for lucre or some private and malicious motive ; to hold a fort or castle against the King or his troops, if actual force be used in order to keep possession, to join with rebels freely and voluntarily ; to rise for the purpose of throwing down, by force, all enclosures ; alter the law, or religion, etc., to effect innovations of a public and general concern, by an armed force ; or for any other purpose which usurps the government in matters of a public and general nature. All these acts have been deemed "levying war." So also to have insurrections to redress by force national grievances ; or to reform real or imaginary evils of a public nature, and in which the insurgents had no private or special interest ; or by intimidation to force the repeal of a law.

"But when the object of an insurrection is of a local or private nature, not having a direct tendency to destroy all property and all government, by numbers and armed force, it will not amount to armed force."—4 Cranch.

In the case of Bollman and Swartwout, in the Supreme Court of the United States, it is decided that "it is more safe, as well as consonant to the principles of our Constitution, that the crime of treason should not be extended by construction to doubtful cases.

"That to constitute the specific offense war must be actually levied against the United States ; to conspire to levy and actually to levy war are distinct offenses." This case recognizes also the doctrine laid down by Judge Chase in Fries's case, that "to complete the crime of levying war there must be an actual assemblage of men for that purpose."

"If a body of people conspire and meditate an insurrection to resist or oppose the execution of any statute of the United States, by force, they are guilty only of a high misdemeanor; but if they proceed to carry such intention into execution, by force, that they are guilty of the treason of levying war, and the quantum of the force employed neither lessens nor increases the crime, whether by one hundred or one thousand persons is wholly immaterial.

" A combination or conspiracy to levy war against the United States is not treason unless combined with an attempt to carry such combination or conspiracy into execution; some actual force or violence must be used in pursuance of such design to levy war; but it is altogether immaterial whether the force used is sufficient to effectuate the object; any force connected with the intention, will constitute the crime of 'levying war.' "

In Mitchell's case it was decided that to resist or prevent by armed force, the execution of a particular statute of the United States, is a levying war against the United States, and consequently treason within the true meaning of the constitution.

And in Fries's case, that " an insurrection or rising of any body of people within the United States, to attain by force or violence any object of a great public nature, or of public national and general concern, is levying war against the United States.

" That any insurrection to resist or prevent by force or violence the execution of any statute of the United States, under any pretense of its being unequal, burdensome, oppressive or unconstitutional, is a levying of war against the United States within the Constitution."

And again, " If the intention be to prevent by force of arms the execution of any Act of Congress altogether, any forcible opposition calculated to carry that intention into effect is levying war against the United States."—U. S. vs. Hoxie, Paine, 265.

But the resistance of the execution of a law of the United States accompanied with any degree of force, if for a private purpose, is not treason. To constitute that offense the object of the resistance must be of a public and general nature.

I do not think it necessary to quote further from the decisions of my predecessors. It will suffice to say that the late charge of my brother Kane to the Grand Jury, in the Circuit Court, contains what I believe to be a correct statement of the decisions on this subject, and that I fully concur in the doctrines stated and the sentiments expressed therein.

In the application of these principles of construction to the case before us, the jury will observe, that "the levying of war" against the United States is not necessarily to be judged of alone by the number or array of troops—but there must be a conspiracy to resist by force and an actual resistance by force of arms or intimidation by numbers. This conspiracy and the insurrection connected with it must be, to effect something of a public nature, to overthrow the Government, or to nullify some law of the United States, and totally to hinder its execution, or comply with its repeal.

A band of smugglers may be said to set the laws at defiance and to have conspired together for that purpose, and to resist, by armed force, the execution of the revenue laws ; they may have battles with the officers of the revenue, in which numbers may be slain on both sides, and yet they will not be guilty of treason, because it is not an insurrection of a public nature, but merely for private lucre or advantage.

A whole neighborhood of debtors may conspire together to resist the sheriff and his officers in executing process on their property—they may perpetrate their resistance by force of arms ; may kill the officer and his assistants—and yet they will be liable only as felons, and not as traitors. Their insurrection is of a private, not of a public nature ; their object is to hinder or remedy a private, not a public grievance.

A number of fugitive slaves may infest a neighborhood and

may be encouraged by the neighbors in combining to resist the capture of any of their number ; they may resist with force and arms their master or the public officer who may come to arrest them ; they may murder and rob them ; they are guilty of felony and liable to punishment, but not as traitors. Their insurrection is for a private object and connected with no public purpose.

It is true that constructively they may be said to resist the execution of the fugitive slave laws, but in no other sense than the smugglers resist the revenue laws, and the anti-renters the execution laws. Their insurrection, their violence, however great their numbers may be, so long as it is merely to attain some personal or private end of their own, cannot be called levying war. Alexander the Great may be classed with robbers by moralists, but still the political distinction will remain between war and robbery. One is public and national, the other private and personal.

Without desiring to invade the prerogatives of the jury in judging the facts of this case, the Court feels bound to say that they do not think the transaction with which the prisoner is charged with being connected rises to the dignity of treason or a levying of war. Not because the numbers or force was insufficient ; but, first, for want of any proof of previous conspiracy to make a general and public resistance to any law of the United States.

Secondly, there is no evidence that any person concerned in the transaction knew there were such Acts of Congress as those which they are charged with conspiring to resist by force and arms, or had any other intention than to protect one another from what they termed kidnapers. (By which slang term they probably included not only actual kidnapers, but all masters and owners seeking to recapture their slaves, and the officers and agents assisting therein.)

The testimony of the prosecution shows that notice had been given that certain fugitives were pursued ; the riot, insurrection, tumult, or whatever you may call it, was but a sudden "conclamatio," or running together, to prevent the capture of certain of their friends or companions or to rescue them if arrested. Previous to this transaction, so far as we are informed, no attempt had been made to arrest fugitives in the neighborhood under the new Act of Congress by a public officer. (Heretofore, arrests had been made not by the owner in person or his agent properly authorized, or by an officer of the law.

Individuals without any authority, but incited by cupidity and the hope of obtaining the reward offered for the return of a fugitive, had heretofore undertaken to seize them by force and violence, to invade the sanctity of private dwellings at night and insult the feelings and prejudices of the people. It is not to be wondered that a people subject to such inroads should consider odious the perpetrators of such deeds and denominate them kidnapers—and that the subjects of this treatment should have been encouraged in restricting such aggressions where the rightful claimant could not be distinguished from the odious kidnaper, or the fact be ascertained whether or not the person seized, deported or stolen in this manner, was a free man or a slave.

But the existence of such feelings is no evidence of a determination or conspiracy by the people to publicly resist any legislation of Congress, or levying war against the United States. That in consequence of such excitement, such an outrage should have been committed, is deeply to be deplored. That the persons engaged in it are guilty of aggravated riot and murder cannot be denied. The assault and murder were wantonly committed after all attempts to execute the process had been abandoned.

This insult upon the laws of the country deserves, and I presume will receive, condign punishment on the persons who shall be proved to be guilty participators in it. But riot and murder are offenses against the State government. It would be a dangerous precedent for the Court and jury in this case to extend the crime of treason by construction to doubtful cases.

The time may come when, with an elective judiciary, dependent on the will of the majority (which is here the sovereign power), may use such a precedent to justify the foulest oppression and injustice, and the tragedies enacted by a Scroggs and a Jeffries be repeated and again sully the page of history.

But I would not be doing justice to all parties concerned in this prosecution if I did not express my cordial approbation of the course pursued by the authorities of the United States and the State of Maryland on this occasion.

This is the second instance in which a citizen of Maryland, in the legitimate pursuit of rights, guaranteed to him by the Constitution, has been foully murdered on the soil of Pennsylvania. As might be expected it created a great excitement and a just feeling of indignation in the breasts of the people of that State.

The Act of 1850, passed to secure them in the enjoyment of their acknowledged rights, has been received with a shout of disapprobation in certain parts of the country. Meetings had been held in many places in the North, denouncing the law and advising a traitorous resistance to its execution ; conventions of infuriated fanatics had incited to acts of rebellion ; and even the pulpit had been defiled with furious denunciations of the law and exhortations to a rebellious resistance to it.

The Government were perfectly justified in supposing that this transaction was but the first overt act of a treasonable conspiracy extending over many of the Northern States, to resist by force of arms the execution of this article of the Constitution and the laws framed in pursuance of it. In making these arrests, and having the investigation, the officers of the Government have done no more than their strict duty.

The activity, zeal and ability which have been exhibited by the learned attorney of the United States, in endeavoring to bring to condign punishment the perpetrators of this gross offense, are deserving of all praise. It has given great satisfaction to the Court also, that the learned Attorney General of Maryland and the very able counsel associated with him have taken part in this prosecution.

And I am persuaded, that notwithstanding the unfortunate and disgraceful occurrence which has taken place and the just feelings of indignation felt by the people of Maryland, caused by it, that this meeting of that State by its representatives here with the people of Pennsylvania, will tend to efface all angry feelings and foster those of respect and friendship between the people of these adjoining States.

And though the duty of punishing the perpetrators of this outrage may have to be transferred, in whole or in part, to the Courts of Lancaster county, we have an assurance, from the activity and zeal already exhibited by the law officers of that county, that it will be performed with all fidelity.

With these remarks the case is committed to you.

CHAPTER XV.

THE VERDICT AND COMMENTS.

THE JURY were out less than ten minutes—just long enough to ascertain that they were all of one mind—and the trial was brought to a conclusion by the verdict of "Not Guilty." Although everybody had anticipated the result, still the announcement of the verdict diffused a general feeling of joy among all classes, save the open partisans of slavery.

The Government officials had been taught that Pennsylvania was not quite prepared to wear the shackles which the slave power had forged for her, and that public sentiment in the land of Penn was not so debased as to willingly allow the incursions of the slave hunter. It was no wonder, therefore, that the friends of freedom exulted, nor that the minions of slavery were filled with disappointment and rage.

Men gathered in groups in stores and shops, or in the streets, to congratulate each other on the defeat of the Administration and its tools in their efforts to revive, in behalf of slavery, the exploded doctrine of Constructive Treason.

The scene in court after the rendition of the verdict was deeply interesting. Mr. Ashmead said that the prisoner was also charged on four other bills for misdemeanor; but as he had passed through such an ordeal, he purposed entering a nolle prosequi on those bills. If the State does not hold him for anything else, I move for his discharge. Judge Grier said that, on motion, the prisoner was discharged. The friends of Mr. Hanway gathered around him in great numbers to congratulate him and his noble-hearted wife upon his escape from the clutches of the United States Government.

JOSEPH SCARLETT.

The trial settled one point beyond all chance of reversal, viz. : That a company of blacks gathered spontaneously together and armed for the defense of their liberties against the operations of the Fugitive law, even though they slay the monster who seeks to enslave them, whatever other offense they may be guilty of, are not to be hung for treason.

We rejoice in this, says the "Pennsylvania Freeman," not because we approve of bloody resistance to that or any other infamous law, but because we do not desire to see such a statute supported by penalties which could not fail to stimulate the business of slave-hunting and fill the minds of the fugitives with despair. We are opposed to all violent resistance of tyranny, but we abhor still more the violence which is employed to re-enslave the fleeing bondman ; and wherever the master and the slave are brought in deadly conflict, our sympathies must be with the latter. For this reason we should regret any circumstance that might give the master an advantage over the slave, or tend to encourage the former and dishearten the latter.

Much as we admire the heroism of genuine Non-Resistance, we prefer the violent opposition to outrage and wrong which springs from the noblest elements of human nature, though in a state of imperfect development, to that craven submission to the tyrant which is not the fruit of high moral principle, but the offspring of degradation or despair. The advantage of the master over the slave, in a conflict of violence, is already sufficiently appalling to the latter without the addition of any new element of terror.

We believe it is the general conviction of candid persons of all parties, who have watched the developments of this trial, that Judge Kane, Attorney General Ashmead, and the other officials of the government by whose means the Christiana prisoners were indicted for the crime of high treason, were guilty of a stretch of power which ought to subject them to the severest public censure, if not to legal punishment. There was no plausible reason for charging Castner Hanway, or any-body else connected with the Christiana affair, with such a crime ; and no one who perused the evidence can fail to at-tribute such an accusation either to culpable ignorance of the law, or a cruel spirit of persecution.

The charge of the Judge to the grand jury, however it may be defended on technical grounds, and on account of its ac-knowledged hypothetical treatment of the case, was after all a supererogatory stimulus to a spirit which deserved rebuke rather than encouragement from the Bench. Its effect upon the grand jury and upon the community was precisely what might have been anticipated. It inflamed prejudices which were before altogether too strong, and fostered a spirit of per-secution in the upholders of the Fugitive law as discreditable to the state as it was injurious to its victims. In spite of all the apologies which his friends have urged in his behalf, the course pursued by the Judge in this matter has fixed a stain upon his judicial character which no ingenuity or skill can efface. For fulfilling the duties absolutely imposed upon him, by his oath, few would have blamed him ; but for transcending his official obligations and seeking to appease the Moloch of the South by a voluntary offering upon its bloody altar, he must incur the censure of his cotemporaries and the indigna-tion of posterity. The day is coming when the names of all who have sought to brand resistance to the Fugitive law as treason, will be remembered only to be execrated, and when Castner Hanway and his associates will be included in the long line of worthies who have suffered persecution for righteous-ness sake, and because they would not participate in the crime of enslaving their fellow-men.

The only man whom the government succeeded in convict-ing is its own principal witness, the miscreant Kline. He has been buried so deep under the weight of his own villainy, that his testimony in the trials yet to come can avail nothing with any honest jury.

The last count in the indictment against Hanway in which he was charged with having "prepared divers books, letters, resolutions, addresses, etc., which he caused to be dispersed, containing incitements and encouragements to fugitives and others to resist, oppose and prevent by violence and intimidation the execution" of the Fugitive law, does not seem to have attracted the very earnest attention of the prosecution. It was hoped that Mr. Ashmead would produce to the Court some of those dreadful "books, letters, resolutions, addresses, etc.," that the country might learn what sentiments are deemed treasonable in this free country, at this meridian of the nineteenth century, and in the building where the fathers of the Republic adopted the Declaration of Independence. We really do not take this omission of the Attorney General kindly, and know not how he will excuse it to the Government. We are afraid that the miller of Christiana may be emboldened by it to attend fanatical Conventions and patronize incendiary papers !

The trial and its antecedents, though necessarily attended with much suffering to the parties held in duress, has yet done much to awaken public attention to the subject of slavery, and to arouse the people to a sense of the responsibilities involved in their political relations to the South.   The imprudent claim of Overseer Brent, that the people of the Free States were not only bound to permit the South to hunt her victims on their soil, but to engage with 'alacrity' in the man hunt whenever a slaveholder gives the word of command, will do something, we hope to open the eyes of our citizens to the degradation to which they are sunk by their alliance with men stealers. At any rate, the trial has on foot an agitation which it will be much easier to increase than to stop, and which must contribute essentially to the triumph of Liberty over slavery in the great struggle now impending. For the victory which the machinations of our enemies no less than our own fidelity and the overruling providence of God, are doing so much to hasten,

we can afford to wait in calm patience and unwavering hope.
/Messrs. Hanway and Lewis, having been discharged by the
United States (the latter on bail,) went to Lancaster in company with United States Marshal Roberts and Hon. Thaddeus
Stevens, under arrest, to abide the action of the State authorities upon any further charges that might be brought against
them. They were required to give bail, each in the sum of
$500, for their appearance at the next term of the court. The
small amount of the bail would appear to indicate that no
very serious offense was to be laid to their charge. It was a
shame, however, that either of them, and especially Hanway,
after the facts of the case had been developed by the trial,
should be further molested. It is perfectly clear that they
were both innocent of all participation in the killing of Gorsuch,
and of everything else that could justly subject them to suspicion or annoyance for a single moment. Why then were they
not permitted, after lying in prison for three months upon a
false and infamous charge, to go to their homes in peace? Mr.
Lewis, it should be understood, was also under bail for his
appearance before the United States Court to answer the charge of
a misdemeanor in violating the requisitions of the Fugitive law./

Joseph Scarlett and the twenty-three colored prisoners were
detained in Moyamensing prison. The indictments against
them for treason, were abandoned; but Mr. Ashmead avowed
his determination to try a part or all of them for the lesser
offense technically called a 'misdemeanor'—or in other words,
for obstructing the execution of the Fugitive law, or refusing
to aid in its enforcement in obedience to the requisition of the
scoundrel Kline. Mr. Scarlett and Samuel Williams were released on bail shortly afterward.

The " Sunday Dispatch " speaking editorially of the affair
said : The greatest judicial farce of the year 1851 is over.
The principal actors have had their jokes, the curtain has
fallen, and the audience dispersed. Castner Hanway, after a
long trial, has been acquitted.

There is one feature in the case of Castner Hanway which deserves especial notice and strong reprobation. It is a striking illustration of a custom which is becoming prevalent among the Judges of our courts, and which should meet with indignant rebuke. It is the modern system of prejudging cases, which have never come up before the Court, upon excited and exaggerated statements of facts which are not proved. The entire judicial farce which has just ended had its origin in the promulgation of unauthorized and extra judicial opinions delivered by Judges Grier and Kane before any legal investigation had taken place. When the news of the Christiana outrage first reached this city, when the aggravated accounts of the transaction were given, the newspapers informed us that "Judges Grier and Kane, of the United States Courts, pronounced the offense of the rioters to be high treason." This startling announcement of a decision in advance was never contradicted.

Having glutted the jail it became the serious business of the Judges to endeavor to sustain the opinions given in advance.

Thus it will be seen, by the evidence in the case and the entire course of the trial, that a great wrong has been perpetrated upon Castner Hanway and all others arrested for treason, in consequence of the Judges presuming to make decisions and give opinions upon the nature of offenses, of which they knew nothing but from excited report.

Nought can ever recompense Castner Hanway for this outrage upon his rights as a citizen. He must bear the costs without any claim for remuneration. It is one of the unlucky accidents of his life that on a fine morning in September he mounted his horse to ride over to a neighboring house to ascertain the cause of a disturbance. For that ride he has been held up as a traitor, fit only for capital punishment. For that journey he has been made the subject of a great legal experiment ; and, like the victims of Procrustes, he has been laid upon the bed of judicial trial, but it is now evident that from the first he was unjustly charged with treason.

We did not think it possible that the men who urged the prosecution for treason, in the face of law and common sense, could possibly do anything to excite surprise, but that superlative act of meanness of Judge Kane, when he decided that witnesses summoned for the defense of Castner Hanway should not be paid by the United States aroused both amazement and indignation. When the question came up for argument Mr. Ashmead resisted the payment of the witnesses, and Messrs. Read and Cuyler contended manfully against the meanness and injustice of refusing them ; but Judge Kane, in the exercise of a discretion which the law gave him, decided that they should not be paid ! It was not pretended, we believe, that the law required such a decision, though it is contended that it did not forbid it. But, independent of all legal technicalities, just consider how base it was on the part of the Government to compel Castner Hanway to pay his witnesses. He had been charged, as the facts exhibited during the trial fully proved, with an offense of which he was entirely innocent—an offense, too, the penalty of which is death. He had spent three months in prison upon a charge which no intelligent lawyer, whose brains were not utterly obfuscated by the sorceries of the Slave Power, could for one moment expect to prove. A poor man, dependent upon his labor for the support of his family, he had been denied bail, and thus not only cut off from all opportunity of earning his bread, but subjected to severe losses from the interruption of his business. His health, too, had suffered severely from the unwholesome air of the prison. After enduring all this, and when he had demonstrated his entire innocence of the charge brought against him, the Court had the meanness to subject him to the liability of toiling for years to pay the witnesses who had been summoned to testify in his behalf. And Mr. Ashmead even had the effrontery to insist that he had been acquitted only upon a mere technicality—that he was guilty in fact, though not in form !

This was an outrage upon justice of which we find it difficult to speak with any degree of calmness.

While Castner Hanway, (as a punishment, we suppose, for not being guilty of treason when the Government wanted a victim !) is compelled to pay his witnesses, even though it shall make him a beggar, Mr. Ashmead is allowed to put his hand in Uncle Sam's purse not merely for his own fees, but for the accommodation of any of the slave-catching tribe whom it was his pleasure to summon to Philadelphia during the trial. The Rev. Mr. Gorsuch, son of the man who was killed at Christiana, who knew nothing whatever of the circumstances, and who was not even put upon the stand, was accommodated by Mr. Ashmead with a subpœna, to enable him to remain in Philadelphia, at the expense of the United States, during the progress of the trial.

CHAPTER XVI.

THE HERO OF THE RIOT.

CASTNER HANWAY, the chief character, in fact the hero of the riot, by reason of his trial for treason, was born in Chester County, Pa., November 16, 1821. His family being Friends he naturally accepted their faith for his spiritual guidance. He received a good education and learned a trade —milling—growing into a fine example of combined industry and integrity. During his life he resided in the county of his birth for more than forty years and was one of the signers of the call for the first Yearly Meeting of Progressive Friends, and a member until his death which occurred May 26, 1893.

In 1878 he took Horace Greeley's advice and went West, locating at Wilber, Neb. It was here that in 1891 his friends from far and near commemorated his 70th birthday in a manner fitting such an occasion, and his friend Jacob T. Stern, late of Iowa, sent him the following beautiful lines :

> "Few of all the sons of men
> Ever reach three score and ten.
> To every one who sees that day
> A thousand falleth by the way.
> I greet thee, friend, with honest tongue,
> Because thou art the good unhung.
> Had fiends and rebels had their way
> Thou wouldst not be with us to-day.
> I greet thee in thy honest age ;
> Thou standest fair on history's page ;
> A man beloved by fellow-men
> When he is three-score years and ten.
> A life well spent, in hopes and fears,
> Has brought thee 'round to seventy years.
> Thy wealth of honor fairly won ;
> Thy head is white, thy labor done.
> Now rest in peace and calm content,
> And muse upon a life well spent.
> Farewell, my dear old honest friend,
> May'st thou be happy to the end."

Mr. Hanway was married three times, his last wife being still living. In early life he was united in marriage to Martha Lamborn, a daughter of Jesse and Letitia Lamborn. During her husband's illness while in Moyamensing Mrs. Hanway faithfully nursed and cared for him, but her health finally broke down and she passed to her final resting place on August 20, 1855.

Some years afterward Mr. Hanway wooed and won Hannah Pennock, a daughter of Moses and Mary Pennock, and a cousin of his first wife. Together they journeyed along in their peaceful manner for several years, but Fate had apparently decreed that Castner Hanway's life was to be other than a bed of roses and sickness again carried off his partner and helpmate on January 1, 1864.

In after years Mr. Hanway once more ventured upon the matrimonial sea, being wedded to a Miss Johnston, a relative of William Freame Johnston, who was governor of. Pennsylvania during the time our hero was undergoing his trial for treason.

By his own request his remains were interred in Longwood cemetery, near Kennett Square, where a large concourse of friends and relatives had gathered to pay a last tribute of respect to his memory. The funeral took place from the residence of his brother-in-law, Samuel Pennock.

With the burial of Castner Hanway ended the history of a man who, when put to the test of a choice between certain imprisonment and probable death, and the upholding of the principles of right and justice, unfalteringly chose the latter. It was an example of principle upon which all young people should look and uphold, no matter what the result.

Thomas Walter, of Philadelphia, spoke on this occasion and among other things he paid the following appropriate tribute : " My friends, this is no ordinary occasion. Our brother is now arraigned in judgment before the highest tribunal of which man has any conception, and again, as though it were the verdict of the Court forty-two years ago, I seem to hear the repeated verdict of the Eternal Court of ' Not Guilty !' ''

At the annual session of the Longwood Yearly Meeting the memorial was read by Patience W. Kent. The following extract shows how he was appreciated by his fellow-men : ''One week ago the earthly form of Castner Hanway was laid in yonder cemetery. A quiet, unobtrusive man, he gave no token that his name was one to conjure newspaper notoriety, or stir the wrathful vengeance of the baffled slave power, as it did at one time. Yet in him, was the stuff of which heroes are made. ' He stood by his colors' when that was all he could do.'' During the ninety-seven days that he was in prison he never once complained. He wrote to his wife from there, ''I do not regret my course ; I have simply done my duty.'' With a nature capable of asserting such a beautiful sentiment in the face of so great mental and financial agony, surely the reward in the Eternal Kingdom would be : ''Well done, thou good and faithful servant ; thou hast been faithful over a few things, I will make thee ruler over many things ; enter thou into the joys of thy Lord.''

CHAPTER XVII.

WILLIAM PARKER'S STORY.

NEXT TO CASTNER HANWAY, the principal actor in the Christiana Riot was William Parker, at whose house the affray, which cost the United States $50,000, occurred. William Parker was an escaped slave, and what he said, even if his complexion was of the ace of spades description, even if it has no romantic interest, must be considered an important contribution to the history of that time. The author of every line of this plain and unpretending account of the life of a man whose own right arm won his rights as a freeman is William Parker. His story is as follows :

I was born opposite to Queen Anne, in Anne Arundel County, in the State of Maryland, on a plantation called Row-down. My master was Major William Brogdon, one of the wealthy men of that region. He had two sons—William, a doctor, and David, who held some office at Annapolis, and for some years was a member of the Legislature.

My old master died when I was very young ; so I know little about him, except from statements received from my fellow-slaves, or casual remarks made in my hearing from time to time by white persons. From these I conclude that he was in no way peculiar, but should be classed with those slave-holders who are not remarkable either for the severity or the indulgence they extend to their people.

My mother, who was named Louisa Simms, died when I was very young ; and to my grandmother I am indebted for the very little kindness I received in my early childhood.

Old master had seventy slaves, mostly field-hands. My mother was a field-hand. He finally died ; but after that

everything went on as usual for about six years, at the end of
which time the brothers, David and William, divided the land
and slaves. Then, with many others, including my brother
and uncle, it fell to my lot to go with Master David, who
built a house on the southeast part of the farm, and called it
Nearo.

Over the hands at Nearo an overseer named Robert Brown
was placed ; but as he was liked by neither master nor slaves,
he was soon discharged. The following circumstance led to
his dismissal sooner, perhaps, than it would otherwise have
happened.

While master was at Annapolis, my mistress, who was hard
to please, fell out with one of the house-servants, and sent for
Mr. Brown to come and whip her. When he came, the girl
refused to be whipped, which angered Brown, and he beat her
so badly that she was nearly killed before she gave up. When
Master David came home, and saw the girl's condition, he became very angry, and turned Brown away at once.

Master David owned a colored man named Bob Wallace.
He was a trusty man ; and as he understood farming thoroughly, he was installed foreman in place of Brown. Everything
went on very well for a while under Wallace, and the slaves
were as contented as it was possible for slaves to be.

Neither of our young masters would allow his hands to be
beaten or abused, as many slaveholders would ; but every year
they sold one or more of them—sometimes as many as six or
seven at a time. One morning word was brought to the
Quarter that we should not work that day, but go up to the
"great house." As we were about obeying the summons, a
number of strange white men rode up to the mansion. They
were negro-traders. Taking alarm, I ran away to the woods
with a boy of about my own age, named Levi Storax ; and
there we remained until the selections for the sale were made,
and the traders drove away. It was a serious time while they
remained. Men, women and children, all were crying, and

general confusion prevailed. For years they had associated together in their rude way—the old counselling the young, recounting their experience, and sympathizing in their trials ; and now, without a word of warning, and for no fault of their own, parents and children, husbands and wives, brothers and sisters, were separated to meet no more on earth. A slave sale of this sort is always as solemn as a funeral, and partakes of its nature in one important particular—the meeting no more in the flesh.

The apologist for slavery at the North, and the owner of his fellow-man at the South, have steadily denied that the separation of families, except for punishment, was perpetrated by Southern masters ; but my experience of slavery was that separation by sale was a part of the system. Not only was it resorted to by severe masters, but, as in my own case, by those generally regarded as mild. No punishment was so much dreaded by the refractory slave as selling. The atrocities known to be committed on plantations in the Far South, tidings of which reached the slave's ears in various ways, his utter helplessness upon the best farms and under the most humane masters and overseers, in Maryland and other Northern Slave States, together with the impression that the journey was of great extent, and comfortless, even to a slave, all combined to make a voyage down the river or down South an era in the life of the poor slave to which he looked forward with the most intense and bitter apprehension and anxiety.

This slave sale was the first I had ever seen. The next did not occur until I was thirteen years old ; but every year, during the interval, one or more poor souls were disposed of privately.

Levi, my comrade, was one of those sold in this interval. Well may the good John Wesley speak of slavery as the sum of all villainies ; for no resort is too despicable, no subterfuge too vile for its supporters. Is a slave intractable, the most wicked punishment is not too severe ; is he timid, obedient, attached to his birthplace and kindred, no lie is so base that it may not be used to entrap him into a change of place or of owners. Levi was made the victim of a stratagem so peculiarly Southern, and so thoroughly the outgrowth of an institution which holds the bodies and souls of men as of no more account, for all moral purposes, than the unreasoning brutes, that I cannot refrain from relating it. He was a likely lad, and, to all appearance, fully in the confidence of his master. Prompt and obedient, he seemed to some of us to enjoy high favor at the "great house." One morning he was told to take a letter to Mr. Henry Hall, an acquaintance of the family ; and it being a part of his usual employment to bring and carry such missives, off he started, in blind confidence, to learn at the end of his journey that he had parted with parents, friends, and all, to find in Mr. Hall a new master. Thus, in a moment, his dearest ties were severed.

I was now at the beginning of a new and important era in my life. Although upon the threshold of manhood, I had, until the relation with my master was sundered, only dim perceptions of the responsibilities of a more independent position. I longed to cast off the chains of servitude, because they chafed my free spirit, and because I had a notion that my position was founded in injustice ; but it has only been since a struggle of many years, and, indeed, since I settled upon British soil, that I have realized fully the grandeur of my position as a free man.

On the day I ceased working for master, after gaining the woods, we lurked about and discussed our plans until dark. Then we stole back to the Quarter, made up our bundles, bade some of our friends farewell, and at about nine o'clock of the night set out for Baltimore. How shall I describe my first experience of free life ? Nothing can be greater than the contrast it affords to a plantation experience, under the suspicious and vigilant eye of a mercenary overseer or a watchful master. Day and night are not more unlike. The mandates of Slavery are like leaden sounds, sinking with dead weight into the very soul, only to deaden and destroy. The impulse of freedom lends wings to the feet, buoys up the spirit within, and the fugitive catches glorious glimpses of light through rifts and seams in the accumulated ignorance of his years of oppression. How briskly we travelled on that eventful night and the next day !

Once in York, we thought we should be safe, but were mistaken. A similar mistake is often made by the fugitives. Not accustomed to travelling, and unacquainted with the facilities for communication, they think that a few hours' walk is a long journey, and foolishly suppose, that, if they have few opportunities of knowledge, their masters can have none at all at such great distances. But our ideas of security were materially lessened when we met with a friend during the day who advised us to proceed farther, as we were not out of imminent danger.

We arrived at Columbia before it was light, and fortunately without crossing the bridge, for we were taken over in a boat. At Wrightsville we met a woman with whom we were before acquainted, and our meeting was very gratifying. We there inclined to halt for a time.

I was not used to living in town, and preferred a home in the country ; so to the country we decided to go. After resting for four days we started towards Lancaster to try to procure work. I gat a place about five miles from Lancaster, and then set to work in earnest.

Those were memorable days, and yet much of this was boyish fancy. After a few years of life in a Free State the enthusiasm of the lad materially sobered down, and I found, by bitter experience, that to preserve my stolen liberty I must pay, unremittingly, an almost sleepless vigilance ; yet to this day I have never looked back regretfully to Old Maryland, nor yearned for her flesh-pots.

I have said I engaged to work ; I hired my services for three months for the round sum of three dollars per month. I thought this an immense sum. Fast work was no trouble to me ; for when the work was done the money was mine. That was a great consideration. I could go out on Saturdays and Sundays, and home when I pleased, without being whipped. I thought of my fellow-servants left behind, bound in the chains of slavery—and I was free ! I thought, that, if I had the power, they should soon be as free as I was ; and I formed a resolution that I would assist in liberating everyone within my reach at the risk of my life, and that I would devise some plan for their entire liberation.

My brother went about fifteen miles farther on, and also got employment. I "put in" three months with my employer, "lifted" my wages, and then went to visit my brother. He lived in Bart township, near Smyrna ; and after my visit was over I engaged to work for a Dr. Dengy, living near by. I remained with him thirteen months. I have never been better treated than by the doctor ; I liked him and the family, and they seemed to think well of me.

While living with Dr. Dengy, I had, for the first time, the great privilege of seeing that true friend of the slave, William Lloyd Garrison, who came into the neighborhood, accompanied by Frederick Douglass. They were holding anti-slavery meetings. I shall never forget the impression that Garrison's glowing words made upon me. I had formerly known Mr. Douglass as a slave in Maryland ; I was therefore not prepared for the progress he then showed—neither for his free-spoken or manly language against slavery. I listened with the intense satisfaction that only a refugee could feel, when hearing, embodied in earnest, well chosen, and strong speech, his own crude ideas of freedom, and his own hearty censure of the man-stealer. I believed, I knew, every word he said was true. It was the whole truth—nothing kept back—no trifling with human rights, no trading in the blood of the slave extenuated, nothing against the slaveholder said in malice. I have never listened to words from the lips of mortal man which were more acceptable to me ; and although privileged since then to hear many able and good men speak on slavery no doctrine has seemed to me so pure, so unworldly as his.

A short while prior to this, a number of us had formed an organization for mutual protection against slaveholders and kidnapers, and had resolved to prevent any of our brethren being taken back into slavery, at the risk of our own lives. We collected together that evening, and went down to the valley ; but the kidnapers had gone. We watched for them several nights in succession, without result ; for so much alarmed were the tavern-keepers by our demonstration, that they refused to let them stop over night with them. Kidnaping was so common, while I lived with the Doctor, that we were kept in constant fear. We would hear of slaveholders or kidnapers every two or three weeks ; sometimes a party of white men would break into a house and take a man away, no one knew where ; and, again, a whole family would be carried off. There was no power to protect them, nor to prevent it. So completely roused were my feelings that I vowed to let no slaveholder take back a fugitive, if I could but get my eye on him.

One day word was sent to me that slaveholders had taken William Dorsey, and had put him into Lancaster jail to await a trial. Dorsey had a wife and three or four children ; but what was it to the slaveholder, if the wife and children should starve? We consulted together, as to what course to take to deliver him ; but no plan that was proposed could be worked.

I was sitting one evening in a friend's house, conversing about these marauding parties, when I remarked to him that a stop should be put to such "didos," and declared that the next time a slaveholder came to a house where I was I would refuse to admit him. His wife replied, "It will make a fuss." I told her, "It is time a fuss was made." She insisted that it would cause trouble, and it was best to let them alone and have peace. Then I told her we must have trouble before we could have peace.   "The first slaveholder that draws a pistol on me I shall knock down."

We were interrupted just at this stage of the conversation by some one rapping at the door.

"Who's there?" I asked.

"It's me ! Who do you think? Open the door !" was the response, in a gruff tone.

"What do you want?" I asked.

Without replying the man opened the door and came in, followed by two others.

The first one said, "Have you any niggers here?"

"What have we to do with your niggers?" said I.

After bandying a few words he drew his pistol upon me. Before he could bring the weapon to bear I seized a pair of heavy tongs and struck him a violent blow across the face and neck which knocked him down. He lay for a few minutes senseless, but afterwards rose and walked out of the house, followed by his comrades, who also said nothing to us, but merely asked their leader, as they went out, if he was hurt.

The part of Lancaster County in which I lived was near Chester County. Not far away, in the latter county, lived Moses Whitson, a well-known Abolitionist, and a member of the Society of Friends. Mr. Whitson had a colored girl living in his family, who was pounced upon by the slaveholders awhile after the Dorsey arrest. About daylight three men went to Mr. Whitson's house and told him that the girl he had living with him was their property, and that they intended to have her. Friend Whitson asked the girl if she knew any of the men, and if any of them was her master. She said, "No !" One of the slaveholders said he could prove that she was his property ; and then they forcibly tied her, put her into a carriage, and started for Maryland.

While the kidnapers were contending with Moses Whitson for the girl, Benjamin Whipper, a colored man, who now lives in this country, sounded the alarm, that "the kidnapers were at Whitson's, and were taking away his girl." The news soon reached me, and with six or seven others, I followed them. We proceeded with all speed to a place called the Gap Hill, where we overtook them, and took the girl away. Then we beat the kidnapers and let them go. We learned afterwards that they were all wounded badly, and that two of them died in Lancaster, and the other did not get home for some time. Only one of our men was hurt, and he had only a slight injury in the hand.

A large reward was offered by the Maryland authorities for the perpetrators of the flogging, but without effect.

Shortly after the incidents just related, I was married to Eliza Ann Elizabeth Howard, a fugitive, whose experiences of slavery had been much more bitter than my own. We commenced housekeeping, renting a room from Enoch Johnson for one month. We did not like our landlord, and when the time was up left, and rented a house of Isaac Walker for one year. After the year was out we left Walker's and went to Smyrna, and there I rented a house from Samuel D. Moore for another year. After the year was out we left Smyrna also, and went to Joseph Moore's to live. We lived on his place about five years. While we were living there several kidnapers came into the neighborhood. On one occasion they took a colored man and started for Maryland. Seven of us set out in pursuit, and soon getting on their track, followed them to a tavern on the West Chester road, in Chester County. Learning that they were to remain for the night, I went to the door and asked for admittance. The landlord demanded to know if we were white or colored. I told him colored. He then told us to be gone, or he would blow out our brains. We walked aside a little distance and consulted about what we should do. Our men seemed to dread the undertaking, but I told them we could overcome them, and that I would go in. One of them said he would follow at the risk of his life. The other five said we should all get killed—that we were men with families ; that our wives and children needed our assistance—and that they did not think we would be doing our families justice by risking our lives for one man. We two then went back to the tavern and, after rapping, were told again by the landlord to clear out, after he found that we were colored. I pretended that we wanted something to drink. He put his head out of the window and threatened again to shoot us, when my comrade raised his gun and would have shot him down had I not caught his arm and persuaded him not to fire. I told the landlord that we wanted to come in and intended to come in. Then I went to the yard, got a piece of scantling, took it to the door and, by battering with it a short time, opened it. As soon as the door flew open a kidnaper shot at us and the ball lodged in my ankle, bringing me to the ground. But I soon rose and my comrade then firing on them they took to their heels. As they ran away I heard one say, "We have killed one of them."

My companion and I then rushed into the house. We unbound the man, took him out, and started for home, but had hardly crossed the door-sill before people from the neighboring houses began to fire on us. At this juncture our other five came up and we all returned the compliment. Firing on both sides was kept up for ten or fifteen minutes, when the whites called for quarter, and offered to withdraw if we would stop firing. On this assurance we started off with the man, and reached home safely.

The next day my ankle was very painful. With a knife I extracted the ball, but kept the wound secret, as long before we had learned that for our own security it was best not to let such things be generally known.

About ten o'clock of a Sabbath night, awhile after the event last narrated, we were aroused by the cry of "Kidnapers! kidnapers!" and immediately some one hallooed under my window. I was then informed that kidnapers had been at Allen Williams's; that they had taken Henry Williams, and gone towards Maryland.

I inquired around, quietly, and soon learned that Allen Williams, the very man in whose house the fugitive was, had betrayed him. This information I communicated to our men. They met at my house and talked the matter over, and, after most solemnly weighing all the facts and evidence, we resolved that he should die, and we set about executing our purpose that evening. The difficulty was, how to punish him. Some were for shooting him, but this was not feasible. I proposed another plan, which was agreed to.

Accordingly, we went to his house and asked if a man named Carter, who lived with him, was at home, as rumor said that he had betrayed Henry Williams. He denied it, and said that Carter had fought for Henry with him, but the slave-holders being too strong for them, they had to give him up. He kept beyond reach, and the men apologized for intruding upon him, while I stepped up to the door and asked for a glass of water. He gave it to me, and to the others. When he was giving water to one of the party I caught him by the throat, to prevent his giving alarm, and drew him over my head and shoulders. Then the rest beat him until we thought we heard some one coming, which caused us to flee. If we had not been interrupted death would have been his fate. At that time I was attending a thrashing-machine for George Whitson and Joseph Scarlett.

It must have been a month after the Williams affray, that I was sitting at home, talking with Pinckney and Samuel Thompson about how I was getting on with my work, when I thought I heard some one call my name.

I called Pinckney and Thompson, and we went out. Marsh Chamberlain met us and said that kidnapers had taken John Williams, and gone with him towards Buck Hill. They had been gone about fifteen minutes. We rode on to the Maryland line, but could not overtake them. We were obliged to ' return, as it was near daybreak. The next day a friend of ours went to Maryland to see what had been done with

Williams. He went to Dr. Savington's and the doctor told him that the fugitive could not live—the kidnapers had broken his skull and otherwise beaten him very badly ; his ankle, too, was out of place. In consequence of his maimed condition his mistress refused to pay the men anything for bringing him home. That was the last we ever heard of poor John Williams ; but we learned afterwards why we failed to release him on the night he was taken. The kidnapers heard us coming and went into the woods out of the way until we had passed them.

Awhile before this occurrence, there lived in a town not far away from Christiana a colored man who was in the habit of decoying fugitives fresh from bondage to his house on various pretexts, and, by assuming to be their friend, got from them the name of their master, his residence, and other needed particulars. He would then communicate with the master about his slave, tell him at what time the man would be at his house, and when he came at the appointed hour, the poor refugee would fall into the merciless clutches of his owner. Many persons, mostly young people, had disappeared mysteriously from the country, from whom nothing could be heard. At last the betrayer's connection with these transactions was clearly traced ; and it was decided to force him to quit the nefarious business.

At last this man's outrages became so notorious that six of our most reliable men resolved to shoot him, if they had to burn him out to do it. After I had sworn the men in the usual form, we went to his barn, took two bundles of wheat straw, and, fastening them under the eaves with wisps, applied a lighted match to each. We then took our stations a few rods off, with rifles ready and in good condition—mine was a smooth-bore, with a heavy charge.

The house burned beautifully ; and half an hour after it ignited the walls fell in, but no betrayer showed himself. Instead of leaving the house by the rear door as we had expected,

just before the roof fell in, he broke out the front way, rushed
to his next neighbor's, and left his place without an effort to
save it. We had built the fire in the rear, and looked for him
there ; but he ran in the opposite direction, not only as if his
life was in danger, but as if the spirit of his evil deeds was
after him.

A short time after the events narrated, it was whispered about
that the slaveholders intended to make an attack on my house.
But as I had often been threatened, I gave the report little
attention. About the same time, however, two letters were
found thrown carelessly about, as if to attract notice. These
letters stated that kidnapers would be at my house on a certain night, and warned me to be on my guard. Still I did not
let the matter trouble me. But it was no idle rumor. The
bloodhounds were upon my track.

The information brought by Mr. Williams spread through
the vicinity like a fire in the prairies ; and when I went home
from my work in the evening, I found Pinckney (whom I
should have said before, was my brother-in-law), Abraham
Johnson, Samuel Thompson, and Joshua Kite at my house, all
of them excited about the rumor. I laughed at them, and
said it was all talk. This was the 10th of September, 1851.
They stopped for the night with us, and we went to bed as
usual. Before daylight, Joshua Kite rose, and started for his
home. Directly, he ran back to the house, burst open the
door, crying, "O William ! kidnapers ! kidnapers ! "

After the fight, my wife was obliged to secrete herself, leaving the children in care of her mother, and to the charities of
our neighbors. I was questioned by my friends as to what I
should do, as they were looking for officers to arrest me. I
determined not to be taken alive, and told them so ; but, think-
ing advice as to our future course necessary, went to see some
old friends and consult about it. Their advice was to leave,
as, were we captured and imprisoned, they could not forsee the
result. Acting upon this hint, we set out for home, when we

met some female friends, who told us that forty or fifty armed men were at my house, looking for me, and that we had better stay away from the place, if we did not want to be taken. Abraham Johnson and Pinckney hereupon halted to agree upon the best course, while I turned around and went another way.

Before setting out on my long journey northward, I determined to have an interview with my family, if possible, and to that end changed my course. As we went along the road to where I found them, we met men in companies of three and four, who had been drawn together by the excitement. On one occasion, we met ten or twelve together. They all left the road, and climbed over the fences into fields to let us pass ; and then, after we had passed, turned, and looked after us as far as they could see. Had we been carrying destruction to all human kind, they could not have acted more absurdly. We went to a friend's house and stayed for the rest of the day, and until nine o'clock that night, when we set out for Canada.

The great trial now was to leave my wife and family. Uncertain as to the result of the journey, I felt I would rather die than be separated from them. It had to be done, however ; and we went forth with heavy hearts, outcasts for the sake of liberty.

At Norristown we rested a day. The friends gave us ten dollars, and sent us in a vehicle to Quakertown. Our driver, being partly intoxicated, set us down at the wrong place which obliged us to stay out all night. At eleven o'clock the next day we got to Quakertown. We had gone about six miles out of the way, and had to go directly across the country. We rested on the 16th, and set out in the evening for Friendsville.

A friend piloted us some distance, and we traveled until we became very tired, when we went to bed under a haystack. On the 17th, we took breakfast at an inn. We passed a small village, and asked a man whom we met with a dearborn, what would be his charge to Windgap. "One dollar and fifty cents," was the ready answer. So in we got and rode to that place.

As we wanted to make some inquiries when we struck the north and south road, I went into the post office, and asked for a letter for John Thomas, which of course I did not get. The postmaster scrutinized us closely—more so, indeed, than any one had done on the Blue Mountains—but informed us that Friendsville was between forty and fifty miles away. After going about nine miles, we stopped on the evening of the 18th at an inn, got supper, were politely served, and had an excellent night's rest. On the next day we set out for Tannersville hiring a conveyance for twenty-two miles of the way. We had no further difficulty on the entire road to Rochester—more than five hundred miles by the route we traveled.

We left at eight o'clock in a carriage, for the boat, bound for Kingston in Canada. As we went on board, the bell was ringing. After walking about a little, a friend pointed out to me the officers on the "hunt" for us ; and just as the boat pushed off from the wharf, some of our friends on shore called me by name. Our pursuers looked very much like fools, as they were. I told one of the gentlemen on shore to write to Kline that I was in Canada. The ten dollars were generously contributed by the Rochester friends for our expenses ; and altogether their kindness was heartfelt, and was most gratefully appreciated by us.

Once on the boat, and fairly out at sea towards the land of liberty, my mind became calm, and my spirits very much depressed at the thought of my wife and children. Before, I had little time to think much about them, my mind being on my journey. Now I became silent and abstracted. Although found of company, no one was company for me now. We landed at Kingston on the 21st of September, at six o'clock in the morning, and walked around for a long time, without meeting any one we had ever known.

On Monday evening, the 23d, we started for Toronto, where we arrived safely the next day. Directly after landing, we heard that Governor Johnston, of Pennsylvania, had made a demand on the Governor of Canada for me, under the Extradition Treaty.

We tried hard to get work, but the task was difficult. I think three weeks elapsed before we got work that could be called work.

Two months from the day I landed in Toronto, my wife arrived, but without the children. She had had a very bad time. Twice they had her in custody; and, a third time, her young master came after her, which obliged her to flee before day, so that the children had to remain behind for the time. I was so glad to see her that I forgot about the children.

When in Kingston, I had heard of the Buxton settlement, and of the Revs. Dr. Willis and King, the agents. My informant, after stating all the particulars, induced me to think it was a desirable place; and having quite a little sum of money due to me in the States, I wrote for it, and waited until May.

Abraham Johnson and I arranged to settle together, and, with Dr. Willis's letter to Mr. King on our behalf, I embarked with my family on a schooner for the West. After five days' sailing, we reached Windsor. Not having the means to take us to Chatham, I called upon Henry Bibb, and laid my case before him. He took us in, treated us with great politeness, and afterwards took me with him to Detroit, where, after an introduction to some friends, a purse of five dollars was made up. I divided the money among my companions, and started them for Chatham, but I was obliged to stay at Windsor and Detroit two days longer.

Chatham was a thriving town at that time, and the genuine liberty enjoyed by its numerous colored residents pleased me greatly; but our destination was Buxton, and thither we went on the following day. We arrived there in the evening, and I called immediately upon Mr. King, and presented Dr. Willis's letter. He received me very politely, and said that, after I should feel rested, I could go out and select a lot. He also kindly offered to give me meal and pork for my family, until I could get work.

In due time, Johnson and I each chose a fifty-acre lot ; for although when in Toronto we agreed with Dr. Willis to take one lot between us, when we saw the land we thought that we could pay for two lots. I got the money in a little time, and paid the Doctor back. I built a house and we moved into it that same fall, and in it I live yet.

I have now to bring my narrative to a close ; and in so doing I would return thanks to Almighty God for the many mercies and favors he has bestowed upon me, and especially for delivering me out of the hands of slaveholders, and placing me in a land of liberty, where I can worship God under my own vine and fig tree, with none to molest or make me afraid. I am also particularly thankful to my old friends and neighbors in Lancaster County, Pennsylvania—to the friends in Norristown, Quakertown, Rochester, and Detroit, and to Dr. Willis, of Toronto, for their disinterested benevolence and kindness to me and my family. When hunted, they sheltered me ; when hungry and naked, they clothed and fed me ; and when a stranger in a strange land, they aided and encouraged me. May the Lord in his great mercy remember and bless them, as they remembered and blessed me.

NOTE.—Since the foregoing pages were printed, it grieves me to announce that the last vestige of the famous Riot house has been removed by the owner of the property, and the only mark left of the great conflict, probably the most important historic event of the County, is the old orchard, which Nature in her magnanimity has seemingly endowed with new life to remain as a monument on the scene of the battle.—EDITOR.

www.ingramcontent.com/pod-product-compliance
Lightning Source LLC
Chambersburg PA
CBHW021119020726
47500CB00003B/830